TALES FROM MY
MUMMY

A haunting anthology of stories from...mummies.

Contributors: Jeanetta DeBoef Anderson - Cheri Badgley
Angel Baker - Jo Anne Costello - William A. DeBoef
Waylan Duane DeBoef - Felicia Evelyn Morales
Dr. Melinda Hammerschmidt - Carrie Kendall - Melissa Neeb
Emily Kelso - Gail Wadlow Maphies - Allisha Reeves
Samantha Lyn Walljasper

Compiled by Author
AMANNDA G. MAPHIES

Publishing Coordinator – Sharon Kizziah-Holmes

Paperback-Press
an imprint of A & S Publishing
Paperback Press, LLC

ISBN -13: 978-1-956806-68-7

CONTENTS

Acknowledgments i

Introduction iv

Chapter 1 1

Spooky Places and Haunted Happenings 1

    Belvoir Poem..2

    Belvoir Winery: A Spirited Weekend Get-Away.................3

    New Year's Eve Spectral Encounter at the Crescent Hotel ...6

    The Girl Ghost of Walker Creek 10

    Peace Church Cemetery 13

    Spooks at the Stanley...15

    An Ozarks Gem 17

    The Spook Light...22

Chapter 2 24

Unexplained and Spine-Tingling Encounters.......................24

    Black Raven...25

    An Unwelcome Guest..27

    The Adventures of Mr. Brown 29

    My Son Saw Things 33

    Waylan's Story 35

    Ghost Hunting Adventures at the Pythian Castle 37

    Smoke Signals 39

    The Old Barn 41

    The Floating Blanket 43

    The Story of Annie Mary 45

    Phantom Cigarettes...47

    The Nightly Intruder..49

    The Wedding Ring Reminder...52

    A Midnight Greeting 54

Chapter 3 57

    All Hallow's Eve 57

    A Halloween Poem..58

    Another Halloween in the Books 60

    It's Halloween 64

Chapter 4 66

    Tickle My Funny Bone...66

    Fall Joke...67

    Mom, Our House is Haunted! 68

The Sc-hair-y Church Ghost 70
A Threatening Intruder in my Home 72
Charles, the Angel Editor 76
Ghosts in the Graveyard 78
Haunted Housing with My Children 81
Lost 83
"Haunted House on Palmer Drive" 85
I Feel Like… 88
Dating a Vampire 91
Don't Say My Name! 95
Madman in the Cemetery 97
Lucky Day 100
Chapter 5 102
Animal Encounters and Messages from Beyond 102
Meow… 103
Hamilton, the Black Cat 104
The Magic of Cats 106
Angel Cat with a Touching Message 109
Yansi 111
A Star is Born… 113
Atlas Orion Wilkins 114
Orion 116
Pondering the Infinite Beyond that Which We Know 118
The Missing Black Dog 120
Misplaced Fears 122
Whoooooo Goes There? 125
The Owl Angel that Visited Me 126
Messenger of the Night 128
Messages from Beyond… 130
A Message from Beyond 131
My Grandmother, the Dragonfly 133
Chuck, My Guardian Golden Retriever 135
Message Out of the Blue 137
Chapter 6 139
Angelic Encounters 139
The Cry of the Loon 140
The Angel in Aisle Three 142
Angels in Santa Fe 144
Entertaining Angels Unaware 146

Unexpected Angels..148
Chapter 7 150
Tales from Another Room...................................150
Mystical Nights 151
The Honeymoon 153
The Aproned Lady...155
The Things We Leave Behind..............................158
Chapter 8 161
Childhood Memories...161
The Empty Swing 162
Dorrie, the Witch 164
Good Intentions 166
Overhearing an Important Conversation 168
A Tribute to Nancy Drew...................................171
Chapter 9 173
Dreams, Visions and Whispers............................173
Feathers..174
Dream, Vision or Nightmare? 176
Sorrow, Sewing and Seven Stairs........................181
Chapter 10 183
Autumn Magic...183
The Beauty of Autumn 184
Transition..186
Moon Child..188
Strange World: A Writing Inspired by the Wolf Moon 190
Don't Wait for Home to be Perfect to Enjoy It 193
The Masks We Wear 196
The Weary Old Barn 199
Chapter 11 201
Tugging at the Heartstrings 201
Forever and a Day 202
From Broken to Beautiful...................................203
Fly High Mom 206
Voices from the Past..209
Love that Defies Death......................................213
Fears of Being Alone...215
My Son's Greatest Fear 217
Overalls in Heaven 222
Blinded by the Light..225

Something Old, Something New 227
One Single Rose 230
Conclusion 231
Contributing Authors 233

Acknowledgments

The undertaking of writing a book is a fairly overwhelming project, especially one's first book. I had no idea where to start, how to continue, and what to tackle next in this seemingly never-ending journey. Thankfully, I reached out to several folks that had more knowledge about this process than me and held my hand the whole way. Here is a list of those folks that I would like to personally recognize for making this incredible voyage find its way to fruition...

Sharon Kizziah-Holmes, my publisher at Paperback-Press.com, was quite simply, *a godsend*. I researched local publishers and Sharon's name popped up. I stewed over the decision for a day or two and finally made the call. I am so glad I did. She held my hand throughout the whole book-writing process. She gave advice and assured me that, despite having no clue what I was doing, it would all work out well and I would have a hard copy of this book baby in my hands in less than a year.

Elizabeth Schierschmidt was also an earthly angel in disguise. She edited the book. The first book I have ever written, compiled, and attempted to make somewhat entertaining. She did such a wonderful job. She made the process easy, fun, and did not push me to make any major changes I did not feel comfortable with. There was no way I was going to put out a first book without a professional editor and Elizabeth fit the bill perfectly. I am grateful for her tireless work making this dream become a grammatically correct reality.

My parents, who have never doubted my wild imagination and childhood dreams of being an author. As an only child, they withstood many years of my outlandish make-believe and 'pretend with me' childhood games. I think they knew, long before I did, that my desire to 'tell stories' would escape the scope of my small family and friend group. My parents' constant encouragement, reading all of my pieces, and showing up on the sidelines to watch my dreams unfold, has not been unnoticed. They are my biggest cheerleaders and I owe so much of my confidence in this huge undertaking to their belief in me. *Thank you, Mom and Dad.*

My sons, Liam and Waylan, not only each have a story in my book, but they are also my great encouragers and inspirations for many of the pieces included in this book (not to mention photos). My life was reborn the day my first son entered the world. Life as a *boy mom* is a new adventure every single day. I am thankful that God chose me to be their mommy, and knowing these two boys, I am quite sure I will never run out of writing material. I love you both; my babies, *Lem-Slim and Way-Way.*

My husband, who has heard me talk about this book non-stop for nearly a year. He has been faithful in encouragement and providing inspiration to finish what I started months ago. He also has a story in this book, which he allowed me to tell, and for which I am beyond grateful. My husband is not an avid reader, yet he takes the time to read my pieces and I will always be thankful that he supports this obsessionate passion of mine for writing. *Thank you, my love.* Now, we can play in the dirt for a while…. before my next irrational and ridiculous project undertaking strikes. *Wink, wink.*

To the authors of this book. I really went out on a limb one day when reading about a compilation of series from several women authors. I thought, 'Why can't I do that?' And then, *I did.* I reached out to writing friends on Facebook to see if anyone with a love for fall and all things spooky, that nearly matched my own, would care to join me on this writing expedition. I had more responses than I was prepared for. Turns out, many women love autumn, Halloween, spooky stories, and campfire delights, just like me! Some of the authors were already friends that I knew and loved. Some have become friends turned family. I am grateful to each and every author that contributed to this book. Their stories transformed my idea and few random musings to the full package I was hoping for.

Thank you for trusting me with your words and giving the world a rare opportunity to glimpse this work of mostly true, and always entertaining, words of autumn-ish lore. I could not be more proud to have the many names written in this book and without each author, this dream of mine would never have reached the surreal reality it has become. I simply cannot wait to celebrate with each and every one of you, near or far, in person or virtual. We are gonna drink some champagne and toast to this monumental event. *OUR first book!*

To all the family, friends, and acquaintances I have met through this journey, *Thank You*. The comments on my writing pieces always touch my heart. An author goes through phases of inspiration followed by uninspired dry spells. Yet, those true followers have always given me hope that the words would once again flow. You have no idea how much your words of encouragement, 'Keep Writing' and 'I felt like I was there', have propelled me forward toward this monumental undertaking. I believe God places special folks in our paths when we most need them. He certainly did that for me during the process of compiling this book. I am so grateful, thankful, blessed, and excited to finally give birth to this book baby I have loved from its very inception nearly one year ago on a chilly fall October morning.

Now, grab a pumpkin spice something (or whatever your chilly autumn evening desire may be) and let's dive right in….

CAUTION: These stories will spook you, make you laugh until you cry, tug at your heartstrings, and possibly make you think twice about being alone, as we may never really be *alone*….

Introduction

The month of October positively fills me with joy. Summer fading away and autumn showing her brilliant colors for all the world (or those who have seasons) to enjoy. I also love the creepy, eerie, mysterious, and spooky events surrounding October's grand finale, *Halloween.*

Kids in adorable costumes diligently seeking candy. School parties full of sugar, spice and a bit of naughtiness thrown in. Church Trunk-or-Treats with each vehicle's trunk transformed into a scary-*ish,* fun, and creative stop for children of all ages to enjoy.

I relish the cool fall nights, the warm bonfires, the hayrides, pumpkins, witches, and goblins. I enjoy the scary movies, the excuse to tell ghost stories late at night, with or without a flashlight, campfires, and woodsy settings in the distance. I appreciate having permission to reach deep inside and release my inner, imaginative, and creative child for a day. A holiday where children and adults alike meet each other on the same playing field and truly let loose, eat sugar, and enjoy the mysteries of the cosmos beyond the world in which we know.

Because of my love for not only Halloween, but this seasonal time of year, I decided to compile a collection of Halloween memories and haunting tales, some are fictional while others are chillingly real. As a group of authors, mostly mothers, I have titled this work, *Tales from My Mummy.*

In this journey of *All Hallow's Eve,* you will read true accounts of hauntings, bone-chilling poetry rivaling Edgar Allen Poe, fictional stories that may or may not be based in truth, and a plethora of treasured Halloween memories, activities, pictures, and adventures. I am hopeful you will find stories in which you relate and tickle your scary bone, as well as your funny bone. Hopefully, these stories will jog a familiar memory long since repressed.

I have included the author of each work, along with where they reside and their contact information, should you wish to reach out to them to find out more about their story or see more of their written works.

Buckle up, it is a wild, spooky, hilarious, endearing, and adventurous ride encountered on each and every page of this book.

Chapter 1

Spooky Places and
Haunted Happenings

Belvoir Poem

by Amannda G. Maphies

When spirits walk among us;
They pummel through the air.
Reliving monumental moments;
In hopes of which to share.

Was it a joyous season;
she cannot seem to release?
Or a tragic situation;
In need of cleansing peace.

Whatever the reason;
Whichever the tide.
I'll meet you in the evening;
Prepared for a spiritual guide.

If I can help you move on;
Or simply listen to your story.
A friend you have in me;
A hope for future glory.

Belvoir Winery: A Spirited Weekend Get-Away

by Amannda G. Maphies

I recently indulged in an amazing weekend experiencing two of my most favorite things: ghost hunting and wine tasting. Three, if you consider the massive amount of cheese, olives, and Italian food I gorged myself upon in Kansas City and the surrounding metro area.

The *Belvoir Hotel and Winery* in Liberty, Missouri is beautifully quaint and ultra-fascinating. Fall is the perfect time of year to visit as the foliage is near peak vibrancy, fullness, and unadulterated beauty. The hotel itself is old, understated, and hosts a monumental level of creep factor. I was impressed by the simplicity of accommodations coupled with a rich history exploding my imagination circuits sky high.

I thoroughly enjoyed meandering through the original buildings (one was an orphanage, the second a hospital, and the last a nursing home) which are overgrown with vines, branches, leaves, remnants of recent and long forgotten parties, and graffiti galore. The disheveled state of the outer buildings adds to the mysterious ethereal atmosphere and leaves one's mind wondering at Mach speed.

The cemetery behind the hotel and outer buildings can be accessed by walking up a partially gravel/grass paved hill. The inhabitants of the cemetery died mostly in the 1800s, with a few possessing older birth and death dates prior to that historic time. The stones are set in perfectly erected lines of twenty or more grave markers. Some names boast modern familiarity, others so historically rare they seem almost otherworldly.

I personally experienced no ghostly apparitions or spiritual encounters.

Yet.

The quiet of this old building, steeped in years of history, was enough to make the hairs on the back of my neck stand at attention with any minor sound or gentle breeze. With debris lying everywhere, it was almost overwhelming to try and make sense of the questionable material left behind from years of unuse in an old, abandoned building.

My favorite part of the adventure was walking amongst the ruins of the old orphanage. It was surreal to view firsthand the handprint with a heart palm sealed in concrete on the entrance to the crumbling building façade. Looking straight into a room once belonging to two, perhaps three orphaned children, imagining the fear they must have felt being cruelly ripped away from the only security a child knows at that age, their parents. Wondering if the child's stay was a happy one, surrounded by kind and loving playmates, or a dreadful experience involving cruelty, heartache, loneliness, and fear, as many orphanage stories seem to play out.

At one point, I stepped over what I thought was the branch of a tree, but upon closer inspection, it was the rocker rails of an old rocking chair. Was that chair used to rock innocent children to sleep coupled with a comforting bedtime story? Was it a sign of safe haven and peaceful tranquility? Or was it a means of dislodging discontent in the life of a precious soul that long ago walked upon this earth?

Chests of drawers, rocking chairs, handprints in concrete, fireplaces, bed pans, pianos, never-ending hallways full of dirt, debris, and empty bird's nests all combined to form a history so rich and full it almost speaks for itself. A story begging to be told and reaching out from beyond the time each building lived in the height of her glory. The past reaching out to touch the present, to tie the binds of *what was* with the reality of *what is*. These moments in time, etched so rich in history, they cannot be erased by the mere passing of time.

I long for a complete version of experiences from the residents of Belvoir...past, present, and future. It will forever remain a special stop on my ever-growing travel log, and I hope to revisit this rambling old estate stuck in the passage of the long-ago, far-away sands of time, yet still breathing life into the present, one ghost-hunting, history-buffing, wine-imbibing, adventure-seeking guest at a time.

New Year's Eve Spectral Encounter at the Crescent Hotel

A Nightmarish Account told by Chuck Wiersch
Written by Amannda G. Maphies

My girlfriend and I had no plans for New Year's Eve. A holiday typically spent with friends was coming up short this year as everyone already had plans involving family, travel, or vacation. We wanted to do something special and memorable. A friend of ours suggested *The Crescent Hotel* at Eureka Springs. There would be a big New Year's Eve Bash, coupled with shopping, mouth-watering food, and plenty of good, old-fashioned *spirits* to ring in the New Year. Little did I know when planning our weekend getaway that the *spirits* would reach beyond the bar into the otherworldly dimension.

We started off in room 318. A cozy, comfortable, inviting room. My girlfriend was in her element and made herself right at home. We had an early dinner at a local Italian hotspot, *Emilio's*, and then reported to the fourth floor at the Crescent Hotel for a previously scheduled ghost tour. On the tour, we learned the history of the hotel, including several accounts of permanent guests, who happened to be spirits, having passed nearly a century before.

That evening, in room 318, neither of us slept a wink. I could not sleep due to the intense pounding and footsteps directly overhead, since our room was located one floor beneath the popular hotel bar. My girlfriend, not typically bothered by noise, could not sleep due to her overactive imagination. She feared shutting her eyes would put her in grave danger of stirring up the supernatural hosts we spent the evening learning about. In turn, reopening her eyes would surely reveal a creepy, ghostlike apparition standing at the foot of the bed.

The next morning, I went to the front desk and complained about the noise from the night before, due to the proximity of our room and the hotel bar. The manager, who was not available at the time, promptly called to apologize profusely for my discontent, forgiving the previous nights' charge and offering to move us to the second floor, *Room 216*. Right next to the infamously most haunted room in the entire hotel, *Michael's Room, #218*.

Of course, I jumped at the chance to change locations, coupled with the prospect of a good night's sleep. My girlfriend, on the other hand, liked the room we had the night before and was apprehensive about changing things up. Of course, once she realized how much money I was saving, she quickly turned her frown upside down and hatched a plan to utilize my *savings* for a special piece of jewelry she had been eying downtown. *Typical woman!*

We retrieved a moving cart and bellhop and quickly packed our belongings, moving a floor below to *Room 216*. We spent the day shopping, eating, resting, watching football, and preparing for the New Year's Eve festivities in the Crystal Dining Room at the Crescent Hotel. We enjoyed a delicious dinner followed by live music and dancing in the dining hall. We decided to go to our room before midnight to watch the traditional New York City Ball Drop on TV. Soon after, we found ourselves in bed…full bellies, exhausted bodies, and slightly tipsy minds.

We both quickly fell asleep. My girlfriend awoke to me *giggling* (her term, not mine) in my sleep, followed by a desperate plea to *stop* and me continually shouting: "No, No ... NO!" Jerked awake by her shaking me and questioning what I was saying, I told her about the most realistic and disturbing dream I have ever had (and *Trust Me*, I have had some doozies).

The dream started with my girlfriend and I in the bed of this very room. We were kissing and laughing and enjoying our romantic getaway. When suddenly, I heard a creak outside the door leading to the balcony. I started, looking toward the door, which slowly opened, revealing the silhouette of a man sitting in a rocking chair, just beyond our room.

The man was slowly rocking and as my eyes adjusted to the dark, I could make out his white face and dark beard. His beady black, lifeless eyes stared back at me without any expression. Yet, the intensity of his stare terrified me to my core. Immediately, I felt this presence was unfriendly and meant us harm. That is when I started shouting: "No, No....NO!!!!" in my sleep.

In my dream, I ran at the lifeless man, wrapping my hands around his throat. As I did so, his face expanded in my hands, much like someone blowing up a balloon. It grew and contorted into an evil, menacing sight right before my eyes. This was when my girlfriend was awakened and proceeded to shake me awake, due to the level and intensity of my yelling.

I recalled every detail in vivid accuracy, an undertaking highly unusual for me as I generally cannot recall dreams unless they involve heights (previously my greatest fear). My girlfriend on the other hand, whose healthy, active imagination requires little encouragement, was chilled to the bone by the account of vision in my dream…more like *nightmare*.

We both knew exactly who the man in my dream was: *Michael*, the philandering, womanizing hotel ghost; the very same man in which we had heard numerous stories on the hotel ghost tour the night before. He fell to his death while working on a renovation project on the fourth floor. While he died years ago, many believe he still inhabits the hotel to this day, with room *218* being the *most haunted* guest room and historical site of his death. There have been numerous accounts of his co-mingling with hotel guests. He tends to be flirtatious toward women, yet menacing and combative

8

toward men.

While Michael did not reach out and touch me or make a physical appearance on that New Year's Eve, he did something much more sinister and psychologically crippling. He invaded my dreams. He manipulated my mind and put his presence in the one place I could not physically escape. The thought of that dream haunts me to this day. Was it coincidence? *Possibly.* An overactive imagination? *Conceivably.* Imbibing too many holiday spirits? *Likely.* A spiritual vision from another dimension? *Feasibly.*

While I may never know the answers, one thing is absolutely certain. Never again will I stay at the *Crescent Hotel* in *Room 216.* I believe it *was,* and *is,* already occupied.

In loving memory of Chuck J. Wiersch, who left this world far too soon, but daily watches over those loved ones he left behind.

The Girl Ghost of Walker Creek

by Jo Anne Costello

Our girls couldn't settle down on their first night at Walker Creek Outdoor Education Camp. They had just met their high school counselors and new bunk mates, so their excitement was to be expected. By 9:00 p.m., however, the other teachers and I decided they had had enough time to socialize, and we told them we were turning out the lights. Everyone should try to get to sleep.

This was the first year in my six years of going to Walker Creek the girls had been assigned to this particular building, a two-story dormitory with a seemingly endless warren of rooms on the second floor. Each room held four or five sets of bunkbeds, and most of the beds were occupied. The downstairs had fewer bedrooms, a kitchen, and a living room. Sydney, a teacher from one of the other schools, and I decided to wait in the living room until we were sure the girls were finally asleep.

As soon as I sat down on the hard vinyl sofa, I noticed the chill in the room. For a mild October night, I was suddenly very uncomfortable. I could see my breath when I exhaled, so I knew I wasn't imagining the cold. Shivering and hugging myself, I hoped we wouldn't have to wait long before periodic talking and laughter from upstairs stopped. Then, we could return to our own rooms in the teacher facility across the campus.

Looking around this strangely unsettling room, I noticed the sliding doors leading out to a back deck were each inscribed with a large letter *S*, right in the middle of the glass. The sight was startling. I knew that Walker Creek had once belonged to Synanon, a rehabilitation program for drug addiction back in the 1970s. Somehow, in this isolated setting in West Marin, Synanon had turned into a scary cult. Whole families had disappeared into Synanon, giving up their worldly belongings and adhering to the decrees of a ruthless and abusive leader. No one was allowed in, and no one was allowed to leave. Children who lived there during the years Synanon existed were raised communally and could seldom communicate with their own parents. After it was disbanded, personal accounts of actual torture and a secret cache of tape recordings told just how horrifying Synanon had become.

After a half hour of enduring the discomfort of the stark living room, I told Sydney I wanted to make sure the girls were sleeping so we could leave them with the counselors. We made our way up the narrow wooden stairs and stood together at the end of the long, dimly lit hallway. Happily, we heard no sounds coming from the rooms, and everyone seemed to be sleeping. Just as we were turning to leave, however, a girl came from a room at the end of the hallway. She was strangely silent and appeared almost somnambulant as she moved toward us. Her white pajamas with the buttoned top and wide lapels were atypical since all our girls wore tank tops and sweatpants or patterned flannels to bed.

"It's a *ghost*," Sydney finally whispered, grabbing my hand. No sooner had she said it than the girl, now about ten feet away, disappeared into the wall. She was simply gone!

The next morning as we ate breakfast in the dining hall after a sleepless night, one of Sydney's students came up to talk to us.

"The strangest thing happened early this morning," she said. "I woke up when it was barely light out, and I saw this girl asleep on one of the lower bunks. I didn't recognize her, and I was worried about her because she didn't have a sleeping bag or even a blanket. She was just lying there on the bare mattress, and she had on these weird white pajamas. But I was so tired, I went back to sleep, and when I woke up, she was gone. Then, when we were getting dressed this morning, she came into the bathroom. She was still in her pajamas, and she wouldn't talk to anyone. She just stood there with her head down like she was super shy. She doesn't go to our school, and really, she looked younger than a sixth grader. Do you know who she is?"

Sydney and I stared at each other. Clearly, this was our little spirit. "She must go to one of the other schools," Sydney mumbled. I nodded.

"She doesn't sound like one of mine either," I said. "But there are three other schools here. I'll ask the other teachers."

Instead of asking another teacher, I went to talk to Stacey, one of the naturalists.

"Seriously," I said without preamble, "is the girls' dorm haunted?"

"Pale little blond-haired girl in white pajamas?" Stacey chuckled although I couldn't see the humor in it.

"Yes!"

"So, you've met our little ghost girl?"

"I guess we have," I answered.

"Yeah, the maintenance men won't even go into the building alone, and especially not the second floor. They're terrified of her! But I've seen her. She's just a lost little girl. That was the children's dorm during the Synanon years. She probably died there from some untreated childhood illness, and she's never left."

I couldn't wait to get away from Walker Creek at the end of the week-long session. After all the time I had spent there with my students in previous years, hiking and exploring the peaceful, bucolic surroundings, the allure of the place had disappeared. I changed grades the following year, so I never had to go back. However, I ran into Sydney one day at a teacher conference, and she told me she had seen the ghost girl once again during the next Outdoor Education session. This time the ghost was wandering the grounds outside the dormitory. So, if she had finally found a way to leave the building, then hopefully she can move on. My prayer for her is that she can find a safe, less tainted place, and embrace the eternal rest she deserves.

Peace Church Cemetery

by Amannda G. Maphies

I drug my fiancé, Justin, on a wild goose chase to Peace Church Cemetery, which I read about recently. This historical cemetery exists on the outskirts of Joplin, Missouri. The old-school Baptist church has long since dissolved to ruins. However, the cemetery, containing nearly as many unmarked graves as marked, remains to this day.

Walking along the gravel path surrounding the outskirts of this *older than dirt* burial ground, an eerie presence cascaded the perimeter. Knowing, from recent research, hundreds of soldiers, family members, children whose lives were snuffed out before they had a chance to shine, and one infamous murderer/career criminal by the name of *Billy Cook,* whose human remains lie hidden in an unmarked grave, I felt the bitter autumn chill.

Or, was it a chill produced by something a bit more...ethereal?

While the history of this place is absolutely fascinating, it is also a visceral reminder that in this life, the real legacy we leave is the lives we touched, the footprint of influence we shared, the love we gave, and the hearts we tenderly touched. Nothing else matters. It all passes away. Leaving one solitary stone to mark the sight of a life once lived...

Some stones boast colorful, poetic words to soothe the living souls of those left behind. Others simply say *Grave* to mark the resting spot of a human body, whose soul has long since escaped this world.

Whether a gravestone displays a name, dates, familial relationships, a beautiful message, or simply reads: *Grave,* each marker signifies a life once lived, a story untold, a legacy that deserves to be shared.

14

Spooks at the Stanley

by Gail Wadlow Maphies

Many years ago, my family took a vacation to Estes Park, Colorado. The three of us: my husband, Duane, my daughter, Manndi, and I stayed at the hotel up in the mountains where Stephen King was inspired to write what would become a classic in horror, *The Shining,* set at The Overlook Hotel.

This historic hotel, The Stanley, sits high up on the snowy peaks of the Rocky Mountains, overlooking the town of Estes Park, Colorado below. The beauty of the white and red hotel façade, set against the pristine snow in Colorado's peak ski season, is truly beautiful! Paranormal activities surround its walls and the land on which it sets. I had always wanted to see inside the *Grand Lady of the West.* Not only did we look inside, but we ended up staying one night at the infamous, known-to-be-haunted, *Stanley Hotel.*

My daughter was school age back then and I cannot recall who was more excited, her or myself? We have always loved the movie, *The Shining.*

The night we stayed, my daughter and I set out to explore together. Her dad wanted no part of the adventure, nor the high price of the lodging we acquired for the night. So, we left him sitting in the room looking at tourist pamphlets, and set out on a haunted adventure of our own.

The countless doors to the many rooms and hallways were fascinating. We wondered what might be going on behind each one.

The elaborate staircases, otherworldly carpets, and the eerie feelings we had as we trekked along inside were just as we expected to feel.

We went outside, which was, by this time very dark, and walked the short distance to the opera house. Work renovations were being done, areas were roped off, but that did not stop us! We went inside. Of course, no one else was in there but us (well, no one that we could actually see).

As I recall, nothing really ominous happened that night or during our stay. However, my daughter and I will always have a fondly shared memory of staying there and wandering the hotel's hallways, landings, swimming at night (in the very cold outdoor pool), and just being together. While it wasn't quite the thrill for my husband it was for my daughter and me, we did have a wonderful trip.

If you like scary movies, being frightened by your own imaginings, and enjoying things that sometimes have no earthly explanation, then maybe you can imagine how we felt the time we stayed at *The Stanley Hotel*.

Did we actually see any ghosts? *No*. But, did we feel spirits all around us? *Absolutely!*

Perhaps, your own imagination can be a very scary place to be. If this historic hotel was creepy enough to inspire the *King of Scary Movies* to write perhaps his best-selling novel, surely there are unexplainable accounts just waiting to be experienced.

An aside...

The Timberline Lodge in Oregon was actually where the exterior shots for the original movie, *The Shining*, were filmed. Aerial shots in the beginning of the movie were filmed in Glacier National Park in Montana on the *Highway to the Sun* Road. Interior shots were at Elstree Film Studios in England.

An Ozarks Gem

by Amannda G. Maphies

The Kendrick House, located at 131 North Garrison Street, just outside of historic Carthage, Missouri, has many a tale to tell. From her origin in 1849, this home has provided a dramatic backdrop for injured civil war soldiers, horses of visiting militia (yes....*horses)*, slaves, family members, and it is even rumored to play host to several resident spirits who like to pay a random modern-day visit now and then.

One hundred and seventy-three years young, this home boasts nearly two centuries worth of historically dramatic stories, just begging to be told. Built in 1849, Kendrick Place is one of the last standing homes that remain in Jasper County, despite tragic fires that ran through Carthage during the civil war.

Upon entering the original home through the front door (which is currently not serviceable due to repairs), there are two large rooms on the ground level. One served as a parlor, with a massive fireplace on one wall and an elegant entertaining piano in the corner on the opposite side of the room.

Directly opposite the parlor, you will find an expansive dining room, which housed a large wooden dining table, another grand fireplace, and built-in shelves showcasing old family heirlooms such as dishes, décor, and other personal effects. The two rooms were often left open, with both fireplaces blazing, in efforts to warm the interior of the dwelling on those chilling winter nights.

During the war, the Kendrick House was used by both Confederate, as well as Union soldiers, as a sick house and militia hospital. The home was even used as a courthouse for a brief period of time, before the present courthouse, located on the square in Carthage, was completed.

There is a large rectangle dining table present in the home today that is said to have been used as an operating table for injured soldiers and countless surgeries in prime wartime. Stains can be seen on the wooden surface, believed to be blood from years of countless wartime surgeries. The table would be moved to the back door, where a bucket would be placed at one end, while the table was propped up on the other end, to collect the mounding build-up of blood and other surgical remains.

Another bit of interesting history is that when soldiers would stop at the Kendrick House for respite or medical attention, they would guide their horses into the large parlor room on the first floor. (They brought their horses inside so as not to draw attention to their military presence at the stately home). There are two large wooden cabinets on each side of the massive stone fireplace in the parlor. The horses were fed fresh grown corn out of wooden drawers at the bottom of the cabinets. There are physical hoof prints embedded in the wooden floor in front of the floor-to-ceiling length cabinets to serve as proof of these large creatures' outlandish presence inside the elegant mansion.

In front of the fireplace in the parlor, the tour guide will likely pull aside the large floor rug, which was known as carpet in the 1800s. There are four wooden planks that can easily be pulled up to reveal an expansive open area underneath the house. This was where women and children would seek hidden protection when soldiers or unwelcome guests entered the home. This underground area served as the equivalent of today's *safe room,* offering an added layer of protection to the homeowners' family members.

Upon ascending the curved staircase to the second floor of the Kendrick Home, you will find two large bedrooms on either side of a large landing/breezeway. The bedroom to your left was the master bedroom. Interesting to note, there is a large wardrobe standing in the corner of the room. At the time, houses were taxed based on the number of doors, including closets. Therefore, in efforts to lower the overall cost of the home, many families chose not to build closets in the bedrooms, but would rather use large wooden wardrobes to house their clothing.

The room opposite the master bedroom is where the children slept. There are currently two full-size beds in this room, along with several other antique pieces of furniture, old-fashioned dolls, and several large, colorful plastic balls, which are used as communication tools for the child spirits said to inhabit the Kendrick House.

In this very room, one of the famous spirited children has been known to stand at the window and pull aside the lace curtains so she could take a peek at the activity outside, much as she did when she lived there in the 1800s. Due to spinal issues, she was not able to run and play outside with the other children.

The breezeway separating the upstairs bedrooms has a door at one end and a window at the other. Oftentimes, during the hottest summer months, the door and window were both left open, and the family members would sleep in the breezeway, in efforts to absorb the coolest part of the house and capitalize on the slight summer breeze on the darkest, and most sultry, of summer nights.

There are several outbuildings on the land adjoining the historic mansion. The original slave quarters, a one room white painted square dwelling, is located in back of the home. Several sightings of the outline of a man in period clothing have been seen in the window. There is also an old hand-dug well and the remnants of what was once a gas station owned and operated on the Kendrick land.

The Kendrick House has been owned by the Victorian Carthage Society since the 1980s. Tours were halted during the Covid pandemic, but there are hopes to open the home for public tours once again so this beloved *Old Lady of the Ozarks* can resume showcasing her marvelous secrets and entertaining stories.

While the secrets of the stately Kendrick House and surrounding grounds may never fully be revealed, the Carthage Victorian Society, along with Dark Ozarks, continues to gently invite the actively present spirits to indulge their audience with snippets from the past.

Of course, you can hardly visit a home nearly 200 years old and not assume there are not ghosts still inhabiting the space. Several spirits were mentioned. The youngest, and possibly the loudest, is affectionately known as *Carrot Soup*, her childhood nickname. Carol Sue, her given name, was the granddaughter of one of the many owners over the years. She tragically died of polio before her third birthday and is one of the resident spirits that never moved out of the Kenrick House.

From the peeling floral wallpaper to the tattered rug barely covering the old wooden planked floor, every corner of the historic Kendrick House holds a multitude of secrets from the past. Secrets, if you are quiet and curious enough, that may just find a uniquely spirited way to reveal themselves to present visitors nearly two centuries later.

Today, the Kendrick House can be reserved for private weddings, family gatherings, and historical events. While public tours have not fully resumed, a private tour can be arranged by contacting Lisa Livingston-Martin via The Kendrick House's Facebook Page.

Whether you are a civil war buff, an aspiring ghost hunter/paranormal investigator, an architectural guru, or simply someone interested in how our forefathers lived nearly two centuries ago, there is something of interest at The Kendrick House for every soul that enters.

Some love it so much, they refuse to leave…

*This piece was originally featured in Ozarks Farm and Neighbor Newspaper in the June 2022 Issue.

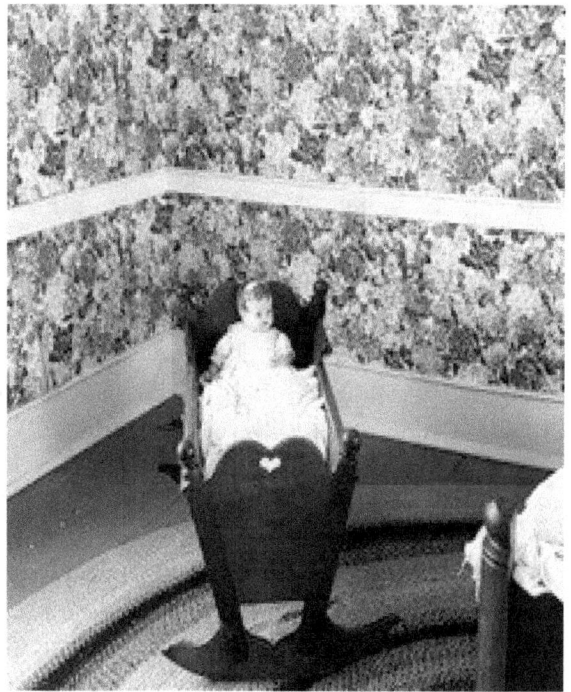

The Spook Light

by Amannda G. Maphies

I attended college in Joplin, Missouri at Missouri Southern State (what was then *College,* but is now *University).* Being a resident of Monett, Missouri, a mere 50 miles east, I was no stranger to the small Ozark city of Joplin.

Early in my freshman year of college, I formed an alliance of friends. Some from my hometown, in which I had graduated high school, and some from surrounding towns where there was a growing-up connection, but we did not necessarily know each other before college. This was a small, close-knit group of young adults, each experiencing our first taste of freedom from small-town, mid-country, Americana life. Our college was known to be a *commuter college* so many local students traveled home on the weekends, leaving the campus lonely and void of much activity.

I cannot recall how many times one of my friends would call from an old-fashioned dial tone phone, in desperate need of a break from studying, and ask if anyone wanted to go see the infamous *Spook Light.* Then, a small group of us would carpool (sometimes taking two or three vehicles) outside of Joplin, across the Oklahoma border to an isolated country road and lie in wait for the spook light we dared to believe existed.

College kids are known for a lot of things, being quiet is certainly not one of them. We were not allowed to legally drink, so we simply got out of our cars, blasted the stereo and danced, listened to music, drank soda or ate fast food, and simply *hung out,* while hoping to catch a glimpse of the mysterious bouncing ball of ... *something* unexplainable.

I never saw the spook light myself. I am honestly not sure I had any friends who saw it either. However, we sure did have fun out on those old country roads. Kids being kids. Before Facebook, Instagram, and video games took over the social desire of America's youth, my generation of college students, my very own friends, parked cars on isolated roads waiting for a century-old legend to reveal itself.

It never did. But that did not stop us from believing, and with each venture, wondering if *this* could be the fateful time we actually encountered the much-anticipated *Spook Light* of the Ozarks.

Chapter 2

Unexplained and Spine-Tingling Encounters

Black Raven

by Amannda G. Maphies

The raven doth sleep;
On a bed made of straw.
Waiting for the next death;
To make contact with his claw.

His beady black eyes;
Full of nothing but gloom.
He plunders the ground;
Seeking his next faithful tomb.

A fresh bed of roadkill;
Lying dangerously near.
He caws that high-pitched sound;
Dramatically stirring up fear.

Content is this scavenger;
To dine on fresh death.
With no shame at all;
He ravages the night.

Landing on a light post;
He slowly peers around.
Turning that craggily head;
In search of destruction upon the ground.

He thinks of little else;
But his next deadly meal.
Revealing his selfishness;
That menacing predator zeal.

He swoops down below;
Refusing to share.
The raven won't rest;
Until he feasts on despair.

An Unwelcome Guest

Account told by Justin Wilkins
Written by Amannda G. Maphies

Years ago, when I was married to my first wife, we lived in an old two-story farmhouse adjacent to a shop, which housed my family landscaping and excavating business. This home was somewhat remote, though located just a few hundred yards from a heavily traveled country highway, with railroad tracks just beyond the highway.

Late one snowy winter's night, while my wife and I slept soundly in our upstairs bedroom, we were awakened by a loud knock at the front door. Of course, our bedroom window did not overlook the front porch, so I had no way of knowing who might be knocking on our door in the early morning hours. I groggily rolled out of bed and headed downstairs to see who might be at our threshold at this ridiculous time of night.

When I reached the front door, I peered through the peephole to see if anyone was standing on the other side. I saw nothing. A bit anxiously, I slowly opened the front door. There was no one in sight. I did, however, notice a pair of shoe tracks in the freshly fallen snow at my feet and beyond the front porch. The odd thing was that the tracks were pointing in the direction of the driveway and heading toward our house. *Yet.* There was no set of tracks *leaving* the front porch. Assuming the person had entered the house, I was immediately on edge. I backed quietly into the house looking for something I could use as a weapon should I need to defend myself, or my possibly trembling wife in the bedroom upstairs.

I searched the house high and low, exploring every single nook and cranny for signs of an intruder. I saw nothing, no evidence proving anyone had broken into our home. I nervously walked back upstairs to the bedroom and reported to my wife that there was no sign of entry and that the uninvited guest must have turned and walked away.

Minutes later, as I was fading back into dreamland, I heard the familiar and chilling knock again on our front door. This time, angry that my sleep was continually interrupted, I bounded down the stairs and furiously opened the door. Again, no one stood on the front porch, where seconds ago, there was a clear knock. Shaking my head, I once again climbed the creaky stairs to our second-floor bedroom and attempted to fall back into a deep sleep.

I spared my wife the information about the snow tracks appearing to travel one direction. I woke up early the next morning after a fitful night's rest and decided to remove those eerie tracks, as I did not want to alarm her.

The memory of those footprints in the snow, coming up from the highway, stopping at our front door, yet never turning to leave our house, has haunted me for years. I have no explanation for the one-sided footprints. However, after that night, I diligently locked the doors before I retired to bed each night.

Though, now that I think about it, I am not sure locking the doors would have kept this entity outside of our home.

The Adventures of Mr. Brown

by Samantha Lyn Walljasper

My dad bought his house with my mom when I was eleven months old. He continued living there after their divorce, until he passed away in 2015. My dad was always a jokester. From the moment he received his cancer diagnosis, he was very firm on one condition: he wanted to die in his home so he could help haunt the place with Mr. Brown.

My entire childhood, Mr. Willard William Brown was a definite presence in our home. We would often hear funny things like footsteps or banging on an old tool bench in the basement during the middle of the night. Every now and then, a sink would randomly be on full blast or a door would suddenly slam shut. Some might have blamed the wind, but we knew better.

The story was that Mr. Brown and his wife, Lydia, lived in the house together until he passed away due to a heart attack in 1972 in the upstairs bedroom, which happened to be mine for much of my adolescence. Lydia continued living there for quite some time before selling the house. She passed away shortly after in 1992. I have honestly never been entirely sure if the heart attack story was actually true or just another one of my dad's tall tales. One thing has always been certain, whether Mr. Brown technically passed away in the house or not, his spirit undoubtedly chose to stick around.

I distinctly remember the first time I *saw* him. It was late and I was supposed to be asleep. Instead, my older brother and I pestered each other until we finally settled down to get some sleep. As I closed my eyes, I heard footsteps in the hallway. I opened my eyes, annoyingly glanced at my doorway, waiting to *whisper* at my brother to go back to bed. Every inch of my body froze upon seeing the perfect outline of a tall, dark shadow in the hallway, walking straight into the bathroom. My dad's bedroom door was still closed, so I knew it was impossible that it was him. Not to mention the sound. I heard such a clear sound of heavy boots on the wood floor, which my dad would certainly not have been wearing in the middle of the night. I quickly closed my eyes tighter than I ever thought possible and pulled my blanket over my head.

I am not sure how long I stayed like that before I got the courage to run into my dad's room to sleep, where I felt safe. Over the years, there were other similar spottings. All equally terrifying, yet oddly exciting. No matter how long it was in-between, each time it happened, my mind would immediately flash back to the first time. It was terrifying but somehow comforting. It felt like I knew I should be afraid, but I never felt like he was a negative presence or like he didn't want us in *his* house.

I think he respected the house as all of ours. At some point, my original belief of not feeling safe, completely reversed. It started to feel like our house had a personal *watchman*. I never doubted Mr. Brown was always going to be connected to my dad's house, but I never prepared myself for the idea he was also specifically attached to me.

In 2016, I went on the Haunted Hannibal Tour in Hannibal, Missouri. It is basically a bus that shuttles you around all the haunted hot spots in Hannibal and ends at the Old Baptist Cemetery, established in 1837 (commonly known as the cemetery from The Adventures of Tom Sawyer by Mark Twain).

We pulled up a little before dusk, and it was as creepy as it sounds. We were instructed to pick up a pair of dowsing rods as we were getting off the bus. They told us to start asking them questions to see where the rods took us. If they opened, the answer was no. If they crossed, the answer was yes, and if they pointed a certain direction, we were supposed to follow them. *Easy enough.*

I started asking handfuls of questions. I asked if I was talking to a spirit buried in the cemetery. Shockingly, my rods opened, meaning *no*. My mind went straight to, you guessed it, good ole' Mr. Willard William Brown. Next, I decided to ask if I was talking to someone who came to the cemetery with me, and received a clear cross for *yes*. Naturally, my next question was: *prove it*. Take me somewhere in the cemetery that will show me who you are. My rods instantly pointed to a hill on the other side of the cemetery. I followed them all the way over and down the hill until they crossed at the bottom. I looked down and at my feet was a grave with the name Lora Brown. Does that sound coincidently close to Lydia Brown, or is it just me? By this point, I was shaking as I asked more questions. I got to the point where I said, if you are really Mr. Brown, take me somewhere in the cemetery proving you know things about my dad.

My dowsing rods quickly pointed back up the hill towards the opposite corner of the cemetery. My heart was exploding in my chest. My hands were sweaty, and it was like everything went silent as I anxiously followed the rods toward the direction they pointed, where I believe Mr. Brown was taking me.

We got close to the far edge of the cemetery and my dowsing rods clearly crossed. In front of me was a small, double gravestone. Some parts were slightly hard to read, but the first names were clear as day. *John and Charley*. Have I mentioned my dad's name was Charles John? That was all the proof I needed to let my tears loose, walk over to what I referred to as *the therapist bench* where the bus driver sat, and turned in my dowsing rods.

I somewhat hysterically shared my experiences, and the bus driver told me it was one of the best stories they had witnessed to date. In all seriousness, I know if you are not a *believer*, this story makes me sound out of my mind. *Could I make this stuff up?* Probably, I am a writer after all … but did I? *Absolutely not.*

I swear on my own dad's grave, which happens to be in the same cemetery as Mr. Brown's, that every word is absolutely true. I believe in Heaven, the afterlife, ghosts, reincarnation, and everything in between. None of us will ever really know what is waiting until we cross over ourselves. But, if there is one thing I am sure about, it is that Mr. Brown is watching over me, for whatever reason. There is simply no other explanation for what I have personally experienced. In some weird way, he feels like family, and I hope he and my dad are really enjoying each other's company.

Samantha Lyn Walljasper resides in Donnellson, IA
Facebook, *Over My Husband's Head*
@lovepoemskindof

Willard William Brown
in the U.S., Find a Grave Index, 1600s-Current

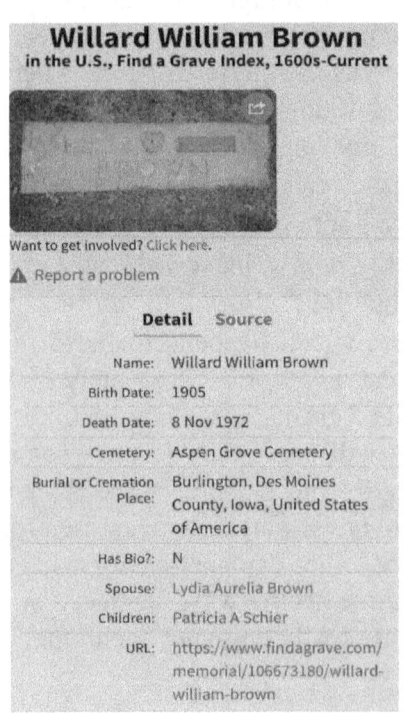

Want to get involved? Click here.

⚠ Report a problem

Detail Source	
Name:	Willard William Brown
Birth Date:	1905
Death Date:	8 Nov 1972
Cemetery:	Aspen Grove Cemetery
Burial or Cremation Place:	Burlington, Des Moines County, Iowa, United States of America
Has Bio?:	N
Spouse:	Lydia Aurelia Brown
Children:	Patricia A Schier
URL:	https://www.findagrave.com/memorial/106673180/willard-william-brown

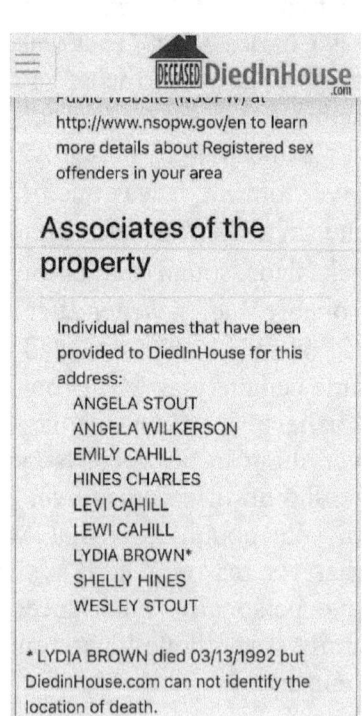

DECEASED **DiedInHouse**
.com

Public website (NSOPW) at http://www.nsopw.gov/en to learn more details about Registered sex offenders in your area

Associates of the property

Individual names that have been provided to DiedInHouse for this address:

ANGELA STOUT
ANGELA WILKERSON
EMILY CAHILL
HINES CHARLES
LEVI CAHILL
LEWI CAHILL
LYDIA BROWN*
SHELLY HINES
WESLEY STOUT

* LYDIA BROWN died 03/13/1992 but DiedinHouse.com can not identify the location of death.

My Son Saw Things

by Cheri Badgley
Carl Junction, MO

When Eric was 4, he went through this phase where he *saw* things – people. At the time, we lived in an old house that had been added on to. The boys' rooms and a half-bath were the addition, and strangely, the part of the house I always felt *weirded – out* in (a part of me still feels bad for making them sleep in there).

One time, the boys were sleeping in our bed, and I was crowded out, so I went to sleep in their room. They had a double bed with a rail on the side and a baby monitor attached to it. I was in that half-in half-out sleep state and felt the foot of the bed being raised. I remember thinking the baby monitor was on so I could yell for Tony, but I could not make a sound. I thought if I rattled the rail, it would make enough noise through the monitor to wake Tony up. Yet, I could not move. I finally *snapped to* and was fully awake, but my entire body was tingling. I jumped up and went back to my sliver of bed and never slept in that room again.

Another time, again, I was crowded out of bed, so I went to sleep on the couch this time…with the light on. One of the boys just had a birthday party and we had a partially inflated balloon still floating around. We had a Jack Russell dog at the time who was sleeping on the couch by my feet. I woke up to him barking aggressively and noticed that the red balloon was floating right by my head and Poker, the dog, was barking directly at it. Again, I went back to my sliver of bed and never slept on the couch again.

Our living room had mirrored closet doors reflecting the creepy new addition and not long after my experience, Eric, around age 4, was looking in the mirror and pointed, asking: "Who's that?" I said, "That's you, silly." He said, "No, right there," pointing at the mirror. Of course, I did not see anything, but I hurriedly took him to another room because I was totally creeped out.

Again, around this same time, the boys were in our bed, and we were getting ready to go to sleep. It was dark, but the TV was on. Eric asked, "What's that?" pointing up at the ceiling fan. We told him it was the ceiling fan. He said, "No, there...it's kids. And they are hanging by their toes. It's scary." Not knowing what to say, I simply said, "When you get scared, talk to Jesus and He will make the scary things go away." That seemed to pacify him, but a few minutes later, he said, "Mom, you're right! Jesus did make the scary things go away! He's standing by you, Dad, and smiling at me!" At that exact moment, something on Tony's side of the bed fell. Tony said, "Cheri, do you have your eyes open?" I said, "Nope, do you?" He said, "Nope."

After this, for the next few weeks, Eric would walk with his hand out, holding Jesus' hand – even walking into the DMV, he was walking with Jesus. It was a precious thing, but it was really creepy how we got to that point!

Waylan's Story

by Waylan Duane DeBoef, 8 years old

This story starts with me having a birthday. I was thinking about what I wanted to do for my October birthday. I decided to go to a haunted house, so I told my mom. My mom told me about the Pythian Castle (Springfield, MO). I was interested, so we went to the Pythian Castle to celebrate my 7th birthday.

We all went into the castle (me, my brother, my mom and her boyfriend). It seemed fun and it *was* pretty fun.

We went into a room at the top of the castle and in this room was a ghost named Petey. He was a child ghost.

I went into the room. I went to the corner of the room and suddenly I heard in my ear, a child's whisper singing, *"Happy Birthday To You, Happy ..."*, then it stopped. I went to my mom; she had her phone on and when I went toward her, her phone turned off (and has been dead ever since). This only happens to people when they are around ghosts. This is my story of me and the child ghost, Little Petey.

Ghost Hunting Adventures at the Pythian Castle

(an additional account of Waylan's Story)

I love this guy's imagination! He spent last evening with a friend. Retelling his adventures was the highlight of my morning. He told of their ghost-hunting adventures in the great forest (of Rogersville). I asked how exactly one hunts for ghosts. I mean, I have seen *Ghost Adventures* on the Travel Channel, but I was not sure if Waylan and his buddy used the same techniques or developed their own ghosting procedures.

He informed me they used masks and flashlights. And, they only hunted *bad* ghosts, because apparently, they are more fun to capture. I asked how he knew when there was a ghost nearby since (I am assuming) they are invisible. He said you feel a powerful surge like wind hit your hand and voila', you have run into a ghost!

He went on to say they failed to find any ghosts, so the hunt was unsuccessful. I guess ghosts are sort of like deer, you have to be in the right place at the right time to encounter one. He then said the chances of encountering ghosts are pretty slim since they do not exist.

I said just because we cannot see them, does not mean they are not there. My son deeply pondered this. I could tell the wheels of creativity were quickly spinning in his little boy mind. He then recalled the little boy, *Petey*, who audibly (only my son could hear) wished him a Happy Birthday at the Pythian Castle, several months ago, in October, just before Halloween. This newfound morsel of past interaction reversed his belief that ghosts do not exist and renewed his hope of a more fruitful ghost hunt in the future.

Funny how we often search for things we say do not exist.
Yet.
Deep down we believe they do, or the search would be meaningless.

Sidenote: My son has told and re-told the *Little Petey* ghost story for years since it occurred at our first visit to the Pythian Castle in Springfield, MO for a Halloween ghost hunt. Every time Waylan tells the story, the details remain exactly the same. He never waivers on the account of this child ghost reaching out to wish him a Happy Birthday. While I did not experience anything the night of the ghost tour, my perfectly working iPhone completely died the next day. I spent the whole morning and afternoon at the cell phone shop trying to figure out what went wrong. The technology gurus had no clue. I believe it may have had something to do with the otherworldly energy, which has been known to affect modern-day technology adversely. Not simply based on this experience do I believe my son. He is a truth-teller and while at times, his stories can migrate to the outlandish and fanciful, this particular account has remained absolutely unchanged despite the countless times he has told it, as well as the years that have passed since the occurrence. I have to say…I believe the kid.

Smoke Signals

by Amannda G. Maphies

It was around 10:30 on a lazy Saturday morning. I was getting dressed, doing laundry, all the weekly chores I had tossed aside for the weekend, in hopes that elusively mythical house-cleaning and chore-enhancing inspiration would strike. Inspiration did not strike. But I was out of clothes, so out of necessity, I had to do laundry.

The boys returned from their dad's house less than an hour ago. They were both in my oldest son's room playing video games. I kept interrupting them to do their own chores around the house. You know, the same daily chores that never change, require daily attention, yet somehow still demand a daily reminder from mom.

It was at my most exasperated moment when the distinct smell of something burning assaulted my senses. It smelled like something was on fire somewhere in our house. I assumed one of the boys was making toast and forgot about it, causing the burnt smell to permeate through the house.

Trying desperately to remedy the situation before the fire alarms went off, I ran from my bedroom to the kitchen to investigate. No one was in the kitchen. The toaster was not on the cabinet, as I expected. There was nothing cooking. Yet, I still smelled the overwhelming scent of smoke.

I asked the boys what they had toasted or heated up in the microwave. They both responded similarly, "Nothing." Confused, I asked if they noticed the burning smell I could not seem to locate. They both looked at each other, then looked at me and simply said, "Nope."

I was growing more desperate with each passing moment, thinking my house was on fire, but unable to locate any smoke, flames, or the source of burning I was sure was growing by the second. I even went outside, thinking perhaps a neighbor was burning leaves or barbecuing. Nothing out of the ordinary greeted me outside the front door.

I frustratingly came back inside, checked the dryer, the oven, the Christmas trees (all three of them). Nothing was overheated or smoking. Yet, I still smelled the very real, very raw, very powerful smell. The boys were starting to think I was losing it. I was starting to think I was losing it.

Then, as quickly as it came, the obnoxious smell vanished. There was nothing. *Nada*. It simply went away. With no rhyme or reason to explain how I was the only one to sense it.

Waylan later told me that perhaps I sensed the smell based on some former tragedy involving a fire in or around our home. Ironically, the thought had already crossed my mind. Yet, our house is not that old and as far as I know, has no history of tragic death by fire. Whatever it was, it was real to me, and to me alone. I hope it was a one-time, bizarre occurrence. But I cannot help but wonder what message I may have missed.

The Old Barn

by Angel Baker, Maryland

There once was a barn in the 1930s, that sat at the end of a long, long lane. Old family money erected its walls, and a man with a vision completed it all. The land surrounding was bought up and added to the collection. Pristine white and filled with fancy horses, the barn became a center for the foxhunting sport.

Over the years, the barn became many things, and with the inevitability of time, came wear and tear. By my time, the barn was decades old and had seen better days. It was still functional, but the walls were sagging, the paint peeling and aged, and the roof leaked in certain places, but it was a cozy, happy place filled with life.

The horses now lived there were a misfit bunch of rescues from various places and circumstances and were the center of attention. In high school and college, I worked at the barn and had heard stories of it back in its glory days, and about the old caretaker who lived and took care of the foxhunting horses housed there in the 1930s. As the stories are told, he always had a cigarette hanging out of his mouth, and lived in the room off the office, now our junk room. I always thought it was a wonder he did not burn the place down.

One afternoon, I was at the barn by myself when I heard the distinct sound of human footsteps at the other end of the barn. *Weird.* I went to check it out but found nothing. Nobody else was in the barn with me, two or four-legged. As I was walking back to the office, I sensed the strong smell of cigarette smoke. Who in the world would be smoking in a barn, I thought to myself! I went to investigate, following the distinct smell of the cigarette smoke. I got to a spot in the back of the barn where the smell was the strongest, but no one was there. After checking high and low, I found that I truly was alone, and chills went up my spine.

This continued to happen for the rest of my years working at the barn, and it would happen every time I was alone. The distinct cigarette smoke would come out of nowhere and would always be strongest in that one spot in the back of the barn, coupled with the sound of footsteps walking around, sometimes following me.

I also began to hear hoof steps as well. Of course, over the years we had our fair share of horses pass away at the barn. Some from old age, some from sickness, and some had more tragic ends, like a barn favorite. Sir Lancelot, who was struck by lightning one night in the field.

When the barn was quiet, no human or horse around, I would hear the very clear sound of a horse walking around on the concrete floor, its horseshoes clicking with each step. The first time this happened I thought a horse had somehow gotten out of the field and wandered back in the barn. Yet, there was no horse in sight, inside or outside of the barn.

I began to accept these noises and smells. Nothing else ever happened. It was a part of the memories of the old barn, a part of its history; the lives that lived there still longing to be remembered.

You can find stories like this at Angel Baker's Facebook blog, *"Stories of a Farmhouse"*.

The Floating Blanket

by Samantha Lyn Walljasper

My dad always wanted a granddaughter. He got his wish, and my daughter was only one day shy of two months old when he passed away from cancer. Even though she spent a lot of time with him in those almost two months, she was still too young when he died to *really* remember him.

When he passed away, we lived in a small two-bedroom house on Lincoln St. with a cemetery right across the alley. The same cemetery where my dad is buried. Living there gave us some peace during the difficult time after his death. We would often joke that he was our new neighbor.

There were multiple times, while living in the house, that it seemed obvious my daughter was *seeing* someone. I remember many times while I washed dishes or performed housework, I would glance over at her. She would appear to be staring at someone, or giggling, as if they were playing with her. As if her precious, baby attention span was intentionally being kept occupied while I was busy.

One evening, when my daughter was around eight months old, there is no doubt in my mind our neighbor, also known as Papa Chuck, came over to visit us. I was rushing around the house getting ready to run some errands. My daughter was in her highchair in the dining room. *Alone.* My son was following me around talking my ears off about his day at school. We were in the bedroom when we heard slight fussing. I quickly attempted to finish up what I was doing so we could get going when her fussing turned to crying.

Suddenly, my son and I both heard a loud thud. My mind immediately told me my daughter had somehow tipped over her highchair. We frantically ran to the dining room, imagining the worst, only to find her perfectly content again, snuggling with her favorite blanket.

Her blanket, which had been haphazardly thrown on the back of a chair that was at the very least, a good three or four feet away. The chair was now on the floor and clearly the culprit of the mysterious thud.

My son and I looked at each other very confused. For as young as he was, even his brain immediately registered that there was no scientific way my daughter could have reached the blanket on her own. It was simply impossible. Unless she was secretly Stretch Armstrong, which to this day has not proven to be the case.

Someone gave her the blanket. There was clearly nobody else besides us in the house (that my son and I could see, anyway). Leaving only one other option…*those who cannot always be seen*.

Sure, it could have potentially been a number of spirits, considering we lived right next to the cemetery. However, something always told me it was Papa Chuck looking over his one and only granddaughter.

The Story of Annie Mary

by Melissa Neeb

I am not sure where we are, geographically speaking. Maybe 15 minutes away from my hometown. It is 11:00 p.m. on a Saturday night in the middle of summer, and I am riding in the backseat of my older brother's car. I am 16.

The car stinks of Marlboro Reds and cheap vodka. Both are passed around casually between my brother and his friends, though I do not partake. I don't know why I agreed to come along.

I am a rule follower.

And easily scared.

This booze cruise is not my bag.

A dead girl's gravesite, in the middle of nowhere, is also not my bag.

I don't know how he heard about this place. *I don't ask.*

The undeniable bass of 2Pac pounds in the speakers. In my bones. I wish he would turn it down. I can't think straight.

We careen and bump down gravel roads going much too fast. When we get to the bridge, we all hold our breath.

The car creeps across the bridge, the headlights flicker and we all gasp. I am miserable. I do not want to be here. I would do anything to be safe at home right now.

My brother snaps the headlights off as we get closer to the gravesite.

It is so dark here. My heart thwacks loudly in my ears. Can everyone else hear it, too?

It is dead calm. There is a stone wall around a patch of grass. We elbow each other and laugh. Someone throws a beer can over. Our bravado hangs heavy in the air ... like a dense fog.

Maybe it will protect us.

I don't look around too much. I am afraid to look. Afraid not to. Something rustles next to me and I jump.

I am ready to get out of here.

I sigh heavily when we pile back in the car. I hold my breath over the bridge, willing us across. I do not want to stall out here, as other teens have claimed happened to them when making this same dreadful venture.

The gravesite disappears into the inky black night. I feel as if she has tagged along, a needy little sister, clinging to the bumper, not willing to be left behind again.

Her fingernails leaving tiny marks in the paint.

Legend has it that on October 25, 1886, little 6-year-old Annie Mary Twente died after being ill with pneumonia and slipping into a coma in her home near Hanska, Minnesota.

She was laid to rest in Iberia Cemetery, which is now known as Oak Ridge Cemetery.

It was said that Annie's mother, Lizzie Twente, had an overwhelming sense of dread and wanted her daughter's body exhumed days after the burial.

Richard Twente, Annie's father, complied and dug up the body with the neighbor's help.

What they found would drive Richard to madness.

Annie's body was not found as she had been placed in the coffin. She was on her side, the coffin covered in scratch marks.

She had been buried alive, awakening from her coma in a child-sized coffin. She suffocated to death.

Overcome with grief, her father created a special cemetery on the edge of the Twente farm for Annie Mary.

He was afraid people would try to come and steal her body, so her gravesite was protected by a stone wall 18 inches thick and four feet tall with an iron gate and a brass lock.

Rumors swirled that he was so paranoid, he would dig up her coffin just to make sure it was still there.

The gravesite and cemetery no longer exist. Years ago, Annie was moved to her final resting place near the rest of the family.

Rest in peace, Annie Mary.

Link to the article referenced:
https://ahauntinglegacy.wordpress.com/2018/09/26/call-me-anna/

Phantom Cigarettes

by Samantha Lyn Walljasper

My mom recently moved down the street from us. She was not necessarily planning on moving, but her new house was too perfect to pass up. She had lived in her previous place for years; an apartment which has been in our family for quite some time. I do not recall the specifics, but my late uncle (who we lost to suicide eleven years ago), originally began living in the apartment before moving to the house underneath.

At some point, my grandma moved into the apartment and then purchased the house and apartment, when my uncle moved elsewhere. Several renters later, my mom moved into the apartment and lived there for about five years.

Her moving out was a bittersweet feeling for all of us. Yet, the convenience of her living close to her grandkids overshadowed all other aspects. We firmly believe my uncle's presence resides in my mom's (and his) former apartment.

My uncle was the greatest guy, always making everyone laugh. One of those *Robin Williams' personalities* you hear about. He was always telling a joke with a cigarette in his hand. My mom never smoked and does not tolerate the smell of second-hand smoke. Although my uncle was a smoker, he did not smoke inside the apartment. Not to mention the walls, carpet, and other surfaces had been properly cleaned, repainted, replaced, etc.

Every once in a while, usually late at night, when my mom was all alone, the entire apartment would become engulfed with the smell of fresh cigarette smoke. Nothing close to the stale scent smokers leave in an establishment.

It seemed as if my uncle walked into the room, sat down at the kitchen table, and lit up a brand new cigarette to chat and tell her jokes while she cooked dinner. Over the years, we considered plenty of other causes for the smoke smell, such as windows or vents being left open, but none of them add up.

The only conclusion is my uncle, my mom's only brother, stopping by for a visit, to keep her company. One of our concerns with her moving from the apartment is that we are not sure if my uncle will know where to find her. I guess we will wait for the first time her new home randomly flares up with the pungent smell of tobacco.

I personally can't wait!

The Nightly Intruder

by Allisha Reeves

It has been said you are more in tune with the spirit world in that narrow space between full wakefulness and deepest sleep. This could be why many people have unexplainable experiences at night. That is what happened to me nearly 22 years ago.

My then-husband and I were staying with his parents, as we were about to move to Maryland for his job. I was around 3 months pregnant with our daughter, and as any mom can tell you, even early in pregnancy, you wake up many times to use the restroom.

My husband always fell asleep watching a movie. Since this particular room did not have cable or satellite, we relied on an old-fashioned DVD, or was it VHS? *Who knows?* After the movie ended, the screen turned blue. Not static or black, just blue. The blue was enough to provide a faint light in the room, to which I was thankful since I was getting up so many times throughout the night.

The house was a single-wide trailer his parents had bought new. The front door was located in the living room. When you came in that door, you could turn right and go down the hallway, where there were two bedrooms located on the left, and a bathroom at the end. If you came in the front door and made a left, you would go into the living room, then the kitchen, next the laundry room, and eventually my ex-husband's parents' bedroom and bathroom.

The trailer was in a newer community, much nicer than my idea of a traditional *trailer park.* I have no idea what had been there before the community was opened. I do know that no one had lived there prior to his parents, which makes the whole experience very out of the ordinary. Many people who research spirits say there can be a residual presence haunting a place they have known.

On the night in question, I woke up, but not with the usual full bladder that had become my *new norm.* You know that feeling when someone is staring at you? A feeling that can wake you up from a dead sleep. I have had this feeling many times, as one of my sons used to come into my room in the middle of the night when he wasn't feeling well. He would just stand over me and stare until I woke up. I would be so startled my heart felt like it would beat out of my chest. That is what I felt on this particular night.

Thinking it was my husband, I turned my head slightly to look over at him. His eyes were closed, and he seemed to be in a very deep sleep. It was at this moment I saw movement out of the corner of my eye. The bedroom door had been about halfway open and when I looked in the doorway, there was a figure. It was tall, human-shaped, but not solid, and looked to be wearing something on its head resembling a cowboy hat.

The figure was blacker than the blackness of the hallway. Some would say it was the difference in light between the hallway and the room, but this blacker than black figure *moved*. It looked as if its hand was on the door and if it had a face, it would have been staring straight at me. I do not recall how long it stood there, staring at me and I at it.

I wanted to scream, but I couldn't. I was completely paralyzed. I wanted to do something to get my husband's attention, but no sound would come from my mouth. I considered reaching over and hitting him, but no matter how hard I tried, I could not move. I might have been paralyzed by fear, or possibly sleep paralysis. This was the only time in my life I experienced anything quite so...*incapacitating*. I could not even close my eyes. I was sure that as soon as I did, whatever it was would do something to me. So, I just laid there and watched it, waiting to see what would happen next. To say I was terrified would be a gross understatement.

After what seemed like hours, but was likely only a few minutes, the figure turned and left the room and began moving right, heading toward the living room. I could hear footsteps as the figure moved, which seemed strange to me, since it floated rather than walked.

The sound stopped after 8 or 9 steps and there was no door opening or any other noises at that point. After it left, my bizarre paralysis disappeared, and I was finally able to move...and breathe.

I grabbed my husband and desperately repeated his name, until I shook him out of his slumber.

I wish I could tell you he put on his super-husband cape and went in search of the mysterious figure. However, he either thought I was completely nuts, or was just as much of a coward as I was. He simply told me to go back to sleep. There was no way in this world that was going to happen after what I had just encountered!

My heart continued pounding as if it was going to tear through my chest and now, of all times, my bladder chose this exact moment to let its presence be known. There was no way in Hades I was going into the dark hallway alone. I convinced my husband to accompany me to the bathroom, sure he felt as if he married a three-year-old, but fear had overtaken any level of pride I had left. He told me that if I *had* seen anything, it was probably someone inside the house checking to be sure all was well.

The next morning at breakfast, I casually asked if anyone had come down the hallway in the middle of the night to use the restroom. Everyone denied being up at all during the night. The front and back doors were both locked when I checked them the next morning. No one else in the house admitted they had seen or heard anything all night.

Was this a dream? Was a spirit trying to get my attention? I will probably never know for sure, but no one can tell me something was not there in the room with me, staring straight at me, carrying a message I still wonder about to this very day.

The Wedding Ring Reminder

by Samantha Lyn Walljasper

One night my mom, husband, and I were chatting about an experience my mom had. She was alone in her apartment and a plastic bag lifted itself off the counter and floated onto the floor. There was no draft or windows open, so we decided it had to be someone *visiting* her. My mother has had countless types of these experiences with my uncle. She also thought it could have been my father, or a friend.

The next thing we knew, we were discussing the past experiences we have encountered with *spirits*. We have all heard each other's stories before, but it is always fun (and spooky) to relive them. All we were missing was a campfire and flashlights.

We accidentally stayed up too late. Realized the time, we said our goodbyes and headed for bed. It had been a long week and we were exhausted. Usually, I wake up several times before morning for one reason or another, but I was dead to the world until my alarm went off. I woke up to the annoying ringtone of an alarm going off on my phone. I reached for it on my nightstand and when I realized what was sitting on top of it…my heart skipped a beat. It was my grandmother's wedding ring. The first thing my grandpa gave me, when my grandma passed away, was her wedding ring, and I cherish it to this day. It fits perfectly on the middle finger of my right hand and I rarely take it off.

My mind raced. *How did it get there? Could I have taken it off in my sleep?* The ring fits too snugly to fall off and even if it did, it wouldn't have ended up perfectly placed on my phone the way I found it. I only remove this ring if I am doing something that could damage it, and I always put it back on afterwards. *How could it possibly have gotten there?*

My husband was half asleep but witnessed the entire ordeal. He was as shocked as I was. We started wondering if my grandma was present for our conversation the night before. We thought back and realized we had not brought her up once during our story telling. It wasn't that we had forgotten about her, it was just that none of us ever had experiences which seemed to be her visiting us … *until now*. Perhaps it was her. Perhaps it wasn't, but no other scenario makes sense to me, having experienced this bizarre situation firsthand.

One thing remains certain, we will definitely remember to mention her the next time we are all sitting around sharing our favorite ghost stories.

A Midnight Greeting

by Amannda G. Maphies

Earlier this week, after an incredibly full weekend of birthday celebration for my youngest son, Waylan, including his first sleepover, I found myself exhausted and craving a full nights' blissful hibernation. As soon as my head hit the pillow, it took barely any time to fall into a deep dreamland of welcome rest.

Long about 3:00 a.m., my elderly Labrador, Lucy, became very agitated. This dog usually sleeps on the floor on my side of the bed. On this night, however, she was restless and walked from my side of the bed to the other side of the bed, then she pattered her little nailed paws through the hardwood of the kitchen and back again. She made this round several times, before I was fully awake enough to realize she needed to go outside.

Warily, I drug myself out of my comfortable, warm, inviting bed, and stumbled through the dark house to open the back door. Lucy, despite her age, ran down the steps and out into the dark of night, I assumed to do her business. Walking like a zombie throughout the kitchen and living room, I waited for her to bark, signaling she was ready to come back into the warm house.

After what seemed like hours, but was likely only a few minutes, I heard the familiar *'I'm ready to come back inside'* bark and opened the door to let her in. She immediately came inside and pattered down the hallway to my bedroom. Hopefully, this would be the last interruption of my much-needed night of rest. *I was wrong.*

An hour or so later, I was again awoken by this restless dog. She was breathing heavily, walking side-to-side in the bedroom, and would come to my side of the bed and put her nose practically in my face. It was the most bizarre thing. Having just been through this routine less than two hours ago, I was now extremely irritated.

Still not fully awake, but enough to know Lucy was not going to stop this ridiculous charade without going outdoors for the second time, I laid there in bed trying to let my eyes adjust to the darkness before I rose to walk through the house.

As I laid there, I heard a distinct child's whisper, *"Hi."* Assuming it was my youngest son, who oftentimes invades my bedroom late at night (or early in the morning) when unsettled and having difficulty sleeping, I looked to the end of the bed, fully expecting my 9-year-old to be standing there, silently requesting entry to my bed.

Only, there was no one there. Puzzled, I thought perhaps he was in the hallway and had not yet entered my bedroom. I dragged myself out of bed and into the hallway, expecting to see a little boy silhouette of my son, waiting for me to comfort him. The hallway was empty. My son's bedroom door was closed. I peeked in to check on him and he was in a deep sleep, softly snoring away. It was evident he had not been awake in hours.

Confused and still somewhat sleepy, I walked into the living room, where Lucy was impatiently prancing by the backdoor. I let her out for the second time in the dead of night and looked around the backyard to see if anything unusual stood out.

The night was peaceful, yet something odd stirred within me. Absolutely sure I heard the distinct child's voice whisper, *"Hi,"* minutes ago, caught between dreamworld and reality, as Lucy was obviously upset by something.

I happened to see a blonde flash of hair (Lucy) drinking dirty water from the firepit and decided to go check her water bowl. Sure enough, it was bone dry. My oldest son is supposed to feed and water the dogs in the evening, so I mentally noted a conversation with him in the morning. I gave Lucy some fresh water, let her in, and for the second time, climbed back into my warm, comfortable bed. Only this time, sleep did not come so easily.

Who...or *what*...was that voice I heard?

Chapter 3

All Hallow's Eve

A Halloween Poem

by Amannda G. Maphies

All Hallows Eve;
That magical time of year.
Where children dress up as monsters;
Adults lightly infuse childhood fear.

The night is typically chilly;
With a terror infused in the air.
The candy is ready and waiting;
Trick-or-treaters go in search of the fare.

What is your costume, young man?
Oh! A scary werewolf!
And your sister is what?
A fairy princess!
You make quite an unfortunate pair.

Would you like to come in;
Try a caramel dipped apple fresh from the oven?
Oh no, you are not supposed to talk to strangers;
How else can you indulge in Halloween lovin'?

The leaves are brightly colored;
Yet falling quickly to the ground.
Looking for homes with front porch lights;
Where other trick-or-treaters abound.

Spooky, howling, screaming sounds;
Are met at every front door.
Could this be the one haunted house;
That scares you from visiting more?

Another Halloween in the Books

by Amannda G. Maphies

As I diligently accompanied my newly nine-year-old son, along with his brother, who is 11, their dad, and my fiancé to the *good* neighborhood (across the road from *our* neighborhood) for trick-or-treating last night, I tried to drink it all in. As my boys are getting older, they are less inclined to appreciate Mom and Dad tagging along while they make their great candy conquest in the coming years.

My oldest, dressed as the white-faced serial killer character from *Scream*, was a bit difficult to keep track of. Not only was his costume 97% black, but apparently this costume was super popular this year, as I counted at least 10 other Scream characters, more than once mistaking them for my son, and became quite incensed when they did not answer me!

My younger son, desperate to be Bigfoot (or *Sasquatch,* which sounds way cooler), had the most adorable costume. However, the top head piece was missing in the shipment, so his head was void of the complete Bigfoot ensemble. Thus, he grabbed an old Santa hat to wear on top of his head. When people asked what he was dressed as, he proudly said, "Santa Monkey!" (He could have at least said *Santa Sasquatch*, which leaves a more creative and endearing vision in one's mind).

The night was close to perfect. It was chilly enough to need a jacket and hat, yet the wind was still, and most importantly, there was no rain in sight. My sons meandered the streets in search of the sugary bliss they could not wait to sink their little boy teeth into. At first, they developed a steady plan of hitting all lighted houses on one side of the street, and then returning down the other. The plan quickly flew by the wayside when their little eyes were distracted by the hordes of other children at each house within view.

I was a nervous wreck, since there were large groups of people, accompanying their children as we were. Not to mention those vehicles and golf carts along the streets. There was even a truck with a trailer and several bales of hay in the back. These folks were hay-riding their way through the neighborhood in search of the calorie-infused gold at the end of the Halloween night's dark rainbow.

If I uttered the words, *"Say Thank You!"* once, I must have said them at least one thousand times. These boys were like ninjas on a mission to out-candy the masses, loudly canvassing the neighborhood, taking in the sights, sounds, and smells of *All Hallows Eve.*

We passed a very dapper looking Beetlejuice at one house, a Will Farrell-esque Elf on the other side of the street, far too many wanna-be Michael Myers, and one very square, very large SpongeBob, which took up nearly the whole sidewalk.

After an hour (which felt like three), we went back to our house where the boys excitedly weighed the contents of their pillowcases (they refused to take the familiar bags we have always used this year).

My eldest's bag was a whopping EIGHT pounds and my youngest's was a mere FIVE pounds of chocolatey, sugary, mouth-watering, and eye-tempting sweet bliss. Minutes after weighing their candy, they both dumped the contents onto the living room floor and proceeded to barter for nearly half an hour over which trades they would make. My oldest has a peanut allergy, so I heard such statements as, "I'll give you my Reese's for your Swedish Fish" and "That's my favorite flavor of tootsie roll pop. If you give me that, I'll let you have this delicious box of raisons I seemed to acquire..." They went back and forth for the majority of the evening, finally feeling pleased with the trades they had made, carefully re-filling their pillowcases full of candy, and no doubt relocating it to a special place, expertly hidden from *Mom.*

I gently reminded each child of the many hours of labor I spent trying to bring them into the world. Not to mention the immeasurable sacrifices I have made as a single mother over the past nearly 8 years. And all for just a little Snickers bar, or perhaps a small bag of Twizzlers. *No dice.* Those two sweet, young, innocent cherubs held tighter to their bags of candy than a Santa Monkey with a banana flavored candy cane on Christmas morning.

I know the days of going Trick-or-Treating with my boys are quickly coming to an end. In just a few short years, they will prefer to ransack the neighborhood with their friends, rather than their old fuddy-duddy parental units.

I have always loved Halloween. The spooky sights, the eerie sounds, the mounds of candy so easily accessible, young children in precious little dress-up outfits, an occasional Mom and Dad dressed up to complete the family theme. The air is alive with a mysteriously enchanting energy.

As all good things must come to an end, I guess when my boys are no longer interested in the trick-or-treating candy raids of their youth, I will elect to stay home and look forward to the gaggle of neighborhood kids stopping by for candy. I noticed last night several of the older homeowners sat outside on their porches, giving out candy, joking with the children who came to their front door, and enjoying the night every bit as much as the kids. Perhaps that will be me someday.

Just because Halloween will look different when my children are grown, does not mean it can't be exciting, mysterious, and eventful from a fresh perspective. And, if I have candy left over, the chances of me indulging in what I bought myself, is far greater than my own offspring offering to share their stockpile with me. *Win-win...*

It's Halloween

by Carrie Kendall

Why did I pay $50
for my kid to wear his costume for two hours?
Because it's Halloween.

Why do I find candy wrappers
In every crevice of this house?
Because it's Halloween.

Why is Michael Jackson's *Thriller*
On every radio station?
Because it's Halloween.

Why are my children asking me
To smell their feet?
Because it's Halloween.

Why do I sit outside in the cold,
Passing out candy?
Because it's Halloween.

Why is my coffee
Pumpkin flavored?
Because it's Halloween.

Why am I wondering
Where to put the tree this year?
Because it's Halloween!

Chapter 4

Tickle My Funny Bone

Fall Joke

by Carrie Kendall

Season

    Dripping

       Falling

        Blowing

You think it's Autumn…

    But it's snot.

Mom, Our House is Haunted!

by Amannda G. Maphies

Picture it. Springfield. 2020. Bedtime.

The boys congregate in my bed to say nightly prayers. I muster all my strength from a *very* manic Monday to try to send them on their way. I notice the younger one (who is generally more than ready to retreat to his own space) seems awkwardly hesitant to leave. He then tells a tale I will never forget.

"Mom. When I was in my room 'awhile-ago' (this is one word in our home), putting together my new Lego puzzle, I kept feeling like something was behind me. I would turn to look and nothing was there. But I sensed something!"

Now, I must admit, my imagination is as active as a young Spielberg, and I am constantly on the lookout for otherworldly spirits visiting from their cosmic realms, but last night I simply wasn't buying it. He could tell by the skeptical look on my face that it was not registering on the belief scale.

He goes on to say, "MOM! I'm sooooo serious! I really did see shadows and it felt like someone was there!" I said, "Are you sure it wasn't Hammie? He looks like a shadow. And he's sneaky." "NO!!!! It was NOT Hammie!" *Sigh.* Meanwhile, Liam, who takes little to no convincing for an excuse to sleep anywhere other than his warm, comfy, cozy, full-sized bed, with eyes as big as saucers said, "Well, I'm not sleeping in my room! If this house is haunted, I'm sure as heck not sleeping alone in the room next to Waylan's!"

Ugh! *Sigh again.* "Waylan, I don't think there are spirits living in our house. First of all, it's not that old. Secondly, no one has died here (yet). Lastly, I am TIRED AND I WANT TO GO TO BED so please kindly go to your room and go to sleep!"

The next part of the story may be a little *mature* for some audiences. Proceed cautiously. That young little offspring of mine looked me straight in the eyes and said, with the seriousness of Clint Eastwood in a Dirty Harry *'Go Ahead Make My Day'* voice,

"Mom. The presence had RED eyes."

Well, that was all it took. I sort of lost my mind. But, judging from the look on Liam's face, who had 150% bought into his little brother's weak attempt to scare his mother into sleeping in her bed, I could tell this was a battle I was not going to win. And quite honestly, I was too weary to try. So, I simply rolled over and escaped into dream world, hoping against all hope the infamous shadowed being *with RED eyes* haunting our home was kind enough to be sure the doors were locked, and the stove turned off.

The Sc-hair-y Church Ghost

by Jeanetta Anderson

A number of years ago, a friend of mine told me that she was able to see ghosts. She informed me there were two who resided in our church. Gertrude and Matilda (she had named them) would sit up in the rafters during church service and listen to the sermons which, by the way, they enjoyed very much. I wasn't sure what to think of her over-active imagination, but who was I to burst her bubble?

Late one evening about a month later, I was in our church sanctuary alone. Everyone knows dark empty churches can be creepy - especially late at night. I was decorating for a Ladies' Tea which was to take place that weekend. The lights were on in the sanctuary, but the foyer and beyond was pitch black. Suddenly, I heard a noise. For some reason my mind instantly transported to my friend's story about Gertrude and Matilda. My imagination began to conjure up all sorts of crazy scenarios in which I was their victim. I mean, just because they love the sermons doesn't mean they obey them, right?

I raced over to the wall and hit every light switch existing in efforts to light up the place like a crime scene. Satisfied there would be no crime in such a bright setting, I went back to work, chiding myself for letting my imagination get away from me. Suddenly, I heard it again. I was not sure what I heard, but I heard *IT*. I thought about my options.

One, turn on really loud Christian music to make the darkness flee and also drown out whatever was going down in the foyer (distraction). *Two*, tell myself the imagination is a wonderful thing, but can also get you into trouble if you let it get away from you, and this is one of those times (denial). *Three*, face it head on and see what is really happening (dominate my fear).

I could not respect myself in the coming days and years unless I went with option three. I gingerly headed out to the foyer to investigate. I peered into the dimness. Nothing. I ran my hand along the wall searching for a light switch. Turning on the first tiny light switch, I confidently hollered, "Who's there?" Crickets. I heard *IT* again. "Who's there?" I commanded more forcefully while inwardly contemplating option number four, RUN FOR YOUR LIFE (defeat).

Suddenly, out of the darkness of the next room a figure emerged. At first, all I saw were teeth. Big, glow-in-the-dark teeth. The second thing that emerged was hair. Huge, black, out-of-control like a cheerleader's mid-air pom-pom hair. As the final image came into view, I simultaneously wet myself while preparing my heart to meet Jesus in person.

And then I saw Percy. Percy was a really sweet teen who loved to help out with the youth group. Usually, he wore his hair in tight braids, but tonight was apparently his "foot loose and fancy free" hair night.

After I harnessed my heart, which had fled out the door ahead of my body, I asked him what in the world he was doing lurking around in the dark. He replied that he had let himself in through the back door with a key he had been given, and he was working on the broken soundboard in the youth room. Still a bit unnerved, I informed him that, in the future, if he comes into the church and sees lights on, he should announce himself. Then I added more forcefully, "and for Pete's sake Percy, comb your hair!"

Still on edge from my near instant heavenly homecoming, I headed to the bathroom to finish emptying my bladder. As I opened the door to come out, Percy leaped at me from the darkness (this time on purpose) and let out a loud "MUAHHAAHAA." I shrieked in terror fleeing the scene. I may or may not have considered summoning Gertrude and Matilda to wreak a bit of ghostly fun of their own on him at a future time!

A Threatening Intruder in my Home

by Amannda G. Maphies

My last year of college, I moved into a house with a friend of mine. Originally, there were four girls, but one had moved out to get married and the other, sadly, was involved in a car accident and was killed. I was engaged at the time and simply needed a place to crash when I was not in class or at my fiancé's apartment across town. My friend graciously allowed me to move in, taking the one bedroom on the main floor of the old house, which was commonly known as, *The Party House.*

This rambling old house was huge, with two bedrooms upstairs, both occupied by my roommates, two bedrooms downstairs, one of which I resided, and the other was a make-shift bedroom/media room with a closet which extended under the stairway.

The room I chose was on the front side of the house. It wasn't really a bedroom per se, though it did have a full wall of mirrored closet doors. The doors to the room were glass paned double doors and it was located just off the living room. There was also a second entrance to the full-length front porch from this room that I used as my bedroom.

I never felt un-safe in this house, as there was generally someone home. However, being old and located on a fairly traveled city street, also across form a fast-food establishment, there was a lot of activity-induced noise outside my windows at all hours of the day and night.

One late evening, I happened to be the only one home and wanted to take a shower and go to bed. For some reason, having a very uneasy feeling on this particular night, I took my cell phone with me to the downstairs bathroom. I was the only person who used this shower as the bathroom upstairs was used by my roommates who lived on the second floor.

Locked safely in the bathroom, I recall hearing a clicking sound just outside the bathroom door. Not thinking much of it at first, until it got louder and more frequent, I finally stepped out of the shower, feeling paranoid that someone was in the house. There was a sliding glass door just outside the bathroom. Oftentimes my roommates or I would forget to put the wooden stick in the door, unwittingly leaving the house open to friends, family, or possible intruders.

Freshly showered and hearing the noise outside, my imagination conjured all kinds of unsettling images. A masked burglar dressed in all black who had come in through the back door, thinking no one was home. A homeless person casing the joint for food or a warm place to spend the evening. A hitchhiker stopping in for a drink of water and to take what he could find from the contents of our collective home. The possibilities were endless. They kept swirling on repeat through my over-active imagination and terrified young mind.

Thankful I had thought to bring my cell phone with me, I called my former roommate, who now lived with her husband on the other side of town. She was a like a sister to me and I knew she would tell me what to do, as I was panic-stricken in the bathroom and scared out of my wits to open the locked door.

She answered the phone and tried to calm my loud whispers of fear as I explained the situation I was facing. She suggested I call 911. I was afraid to do that, for some bizarre reason. I was hoping she would jump in her car (or send her husband over) to inspect the house and rescue me from the bathroom in which I felt like a caged animal.

She was not letting go of the idea that I should call the police, so I finally decided (without telling her) to take my chances opening the door and deal with whatever was making such a racket in the kitchen. We hung up and I crept near the locked door to put my ear next to the wood and try to see if I heard anything new. The muffled scraping sounds had died down somewhat, but the eerie feeling that I was not alone in this massive house refused to pass.

Deciding to open the door and confront the intruder sounded legit when I was on the phone with my friend, but now I felt alone again. Without her on the other end of the line, I started panicking. I sat on the toilet for what seemed like years but was really only a few minutes.

The next thing I remember was hearing the unmistakable

sounds of sirens…just outside the door where I sat. *How could that be?* I had not called the police! My phone rang at that moment, and I looked to see who it was. It was my friend, calling to say *she* had called the police and they should arrive shortly. She said it was safe for me to leave the bathroom when I heard them pound on the door (she had communicated to them where I was located).

Beyond embarrassed, yet strangely thankful she had made the call and it was safe for me to exit the bathroom, I, once again, crept to the door, slowly turned the lock, and peered around the corner. With sirens swirling and screeching just beyond the back door of the kitchen in which I stood, I saw movement out of the corner of my eye.

Right by the sliding glass doors, batting at the long, plastic, white blinds, was my roommate's cat. Everything clicked into place in one solitary moment. It was the *CAT* I heard making sounds outside the bathroom! He was playing with the hanging blinds and making bizarre scratching, pounding, batting noises, which I assumed was an intruder gingerly plotting my demise. *That stupid cat!* Instant relief cloaked itself around my formerly panicked body…until I realized the police were in the process of breaking into my front door. *CRAP!*

I rushed to the living room just in time to meet the police. I held my hands up in a show of non-threat and told them I was the one my former roommate had called about. And that I had finally come out of the bathroom to find my roommate's cat, otherwise known as the violent offender I was concerned was trying to kill me. The police were very forgiving as they could tell I was humiliated. They offered to search the entire house, simply because they were there, and I guess it was a low-crime night and they had nothing better to do.

As the police searched my college home, I sat on the living room couch, with my head shamefully between my hands as I bent over and peered at the worn carpet on the floor. I was relieved, humiliated, mildly entertained, and infuriated, all at once. Little did I know that someday…this would be a great story! On that night, however, I was simply ready for the police to leave my home so I could lose myself in the safe, warm, cozy flannel sheets of my twin-sized college bed in the adjacent room.

I do not know what happened to the cat, if he is still living or not, but he definitely used up one of his nine lives that night (not to mention several years he likely shaved off my own young life). My anger toward him, coupled with the police searching for the villain, which turned out to be a young, male, orange tabby cat with a very curious desire to cause havoc, lives in infamy as one of the many stories that old house in Webb City, Missouri could tell…

Charles, the Angel Editor

by Amannda G. Maphies

If you know me, you know I have a passion for writing and share pretty much everything with my small piece of the world. It is no doubt too much for some. But those *fans* who faithfully read my posts and like or comment on them, your encouragement means the world to me. I can scarcely begin to explain how many pieces I have submitted for publication. And how many rejection emails I have received in turn. Many publishers do not even have the decency to properly reject writers. They just leave you meandering in the great wide abyss of possibility, hoping, praying, longing, and creatively *starving* to hear *something*.

You can imagine my surprise yesterday morning when I opened my email to find a message written exactly as follows (yes, even all caps): "THIS IS A MESSAGE FROM CHARLES." Stunned, because obviously Chuck was on my mind (he was *Charles* to many, including his beloved Mother). For a brief moment, I thought perhaps he had somehow, some way, hacked into Heaven's central circuit system, reached out from the great beyond and sent me an email. Trust me, if anyone could get the job done, it was Chuck (or he would more likely pay someone to do it. Is there currency in Heaven)? *I digress…*

Turns out, the message was from a Canadian Literary Journal, *Fleas on the Dog*. One of the Senior Editors was named *Charles* (hence the cryptic, *Ghost* movie-esque (I would have preferred a romantic pottery scene with Patrick Swayze, but beggars can't be choosers) message that read: *'This is a Message from Charles'*, only in all caps.

Charles' (also my grandfather's name, from whom I no doubt inherited my writing chops, or rather perceived writing chops) email went on to inform me that, even though my submission was somewhat quirky and non-traditional (I was in a really bad mood and may have inadvertently released my frustration and impatience regarding the submission and publication process when I sent these two particular pieces), the Canadian journal loved the two works I submitted and wanted my permission to publish them both.

I nearly fell out of my chair. Tears immediately sprang to my eyes. I stood up and humbly started reciting my acceptance speech written in 1998.

For me to receive *that* particular email on *that* particular day is *no doubt* a message from beyond. I get that some of my perceived *messages from beyond* have been a bit of a reach (with a very long arm and an extended selfie stick). But *this* message, from an editor named *Charles*, recognizing my work, enjoying my work, even complimenting me on the tongue-in-cheek title of one of the pieces…this was definitely *no* coincidence.

Of course, I told this Canadian Editor my whole lifelong saga (he then proceeded to deny my publishing rights and block me from email forever). *Kidding!*

After explaining how much his email, in such a fateful, timely, and destined way, without a shadow of a doubt, *MADE MY FREAKING DAY*, his reply was simply, *"Serendipity is alive and well."* How apropos…and author-esque…the perfect response.

Yes, Chuck, Charles, and the Country of Canada, it certainly is…

Ghosts in the Graveyard

by Jeanetta DeBoef Anderson

I attended a small Christian college located in an even smaller town. Since entertainment around town was limited, and the college was extremely conservative, a lot of creative events took place. There was an initiation tradition for Freshman students which included a game called, *Ghosts in the Graveyard*. The rules of engagement were as follows:

1. Separate into two groups - gals vs guys. Guys drive. Gals walk *(it wasn't far)*.
2. Head to the local graveyard on a full-moon night.
3. Guys park at the edge of the graveyard and wait.
4. Gals disperse amongst the gravestones and wait.
5. Once it appears the gals have settled in amongst the gravestones, guys give a silent signal and simultaneously begin honking their horns.
6. Upon the sounding of the horn, the objective is for the gals to make it back to the row of vehicles at the edge of the graveyard without being tagged by a guy.

A couple of girlfriends and I decided to huddle together behind a particularly large tombstone. Having the reputation of *"entertaining class clown,"* partly because I love a good audience and partly to mask my fear, I began a spirited rendition of every truly spooky event that had ever happened to me. As is common when telling a story, I was both physically and emotionally invested, trying with all my storytelling might to terrify my audience. After all, we were in the perfect setting - graveyard, full moon, middle of nowhere - you get the picture.

Being deeply engrossed in my story, the sound of the horn took me by surprise. I screamed as though an ax murderer with evil eyes and laugh was inches from my face. This terrified my audience more than the horn. They shot out of their hiding place and began fleeing the scene (aka *me*). This got me so tickled I forgot my terror as tears began running down my cheeks and legs. Once I had composed myself, I began stealthily making my way to the edge of the graveyard. Miraculously, I made it back without getting tagged.

Surprised and relieved I had made it back before anyone else, I decided to squat in a cornfield across the road and finish emptying my bladder. I was quick and successful. I triumphantly returned to the vehicles as guys began trickling in with their prizes. What a fun and entertaining night it had been for me!

The next day I had multiple guys walk past me offering a greeting and smile. Usually, guys didn't pay much attention to me. *"Hmm,"* I thought to myself, *"I must look extra good today."*

Suddenly the realization for my fame dawned on me. I had been the first, and possibly the only one, who made it back without being tagged! I had gained the attention and respect of nearly every guy at this tiny school! This was good. *Very good.* Pleased and proud, I began to strut down the halls like a *she-cock* (female peacock).

At the end of my final class of the day, another guy approached me. "Last night was great," he offered. "It was great!" I replied. Then I began bragging (as if he didn't already know) about how I had made it back unscathed to the vehicles! "I heard," he replied. "It must have been easy with such a full moon," he said with a smug smirk. Indignant that he did not understand how a full moon makes it harder, not easier, I opened my mouth to educate him. But he had gathered up his things to begin his arrogant (and shameful) exit. As he began walking away, he added, "I hear there were two moons out last night," and then he winked at me and walked off.

My look of indignant confusion turned to horror as realization set in. Someone had spotted me by the light of the full moon, coping a squat in the field! Mortified that I had obviously strutted more of my stuff than I had planned (thus the source of my instant fame), my *she-cock* strut turned into a full-fledged hall-of-shame-waddle as I raced to my dorm room.

My roommate, who was supposed to be a comforting counselor in such circumstances, was still sore about being scared out of her wits by me *and* being one of the first to get tagged. She was certain I had gotten what I deserved. My walk of shame continued for the rest of the semester, and I have never attended a class reunion for fear of being nominated, *"Moonchild of the Corn."*

Haunted Housing with My Children

by Amannda G. Maphies

Some may question my parenting decision to take my kids to a local spook house. *Heck, I question my decision!* However, I assure you, the boys, including my fiancé, Justin, handled the frights infinitely better than their mother/fiancé…

Waylan, my nearly 9-year-old, was more excited than I can explain at the prospect of walking through this old abandoned four-room schoolhouse, where Justin actually attended grades 4-6 as a young boy.

Liam, the apple that does not fall far from my own tree, was skeptical. I had mixed emotions. I knew it would produce perfect writing material for my Halloween compilation book. However, I do not particularly appreciate being mauled by clowns, men with chainsaws, and screaming girls who look like they escaped from the set of *Girl, Interrupted.*

Yet.

I went. I am not sure how it came to be that the most skeptical of our group (Liam, 11), ended up in front. I held onto that child like my life depended on it. He may actually have bruises I held so tightly to his arms, shirt, head, whatever I could manage to grasp to calm my own anxious nerves as we turned every dark corner of that old, abandoned schoolhouse.

In a surprising turn of events, my oldest son was very protective of his mother. He entered each dark tunnel and fog-filled staircase with the courage of a lion. He confronted the dark, masked, made-up creatures with unprecedented gusto. He withstood my hands trembling on his shoulders for the entirety of the tour. I may have even, in my fear-induced state, said, *"Take him,"* as an offering, in hopes the ridiculous macabre monsters would stop screaming in my ear and creepily uttering my name.

Waylan, my youngest, was far from protective. He saw fit to jump from every corner and scare me, more than the paid actors.

He continually uttered my name in a high-pitched creepy decibel that was anything but pleasant. He even attempted to join forces with the evil villains lying in wait, to disclose my name, rank, and serial number.

This young child, one I bore from my own womb, was dead set on providing the thrills and chills our $13/person ensured. This experience was definitely one for the books. *MY book, this* very book, coming soon, Halloween 2022. *Stay tuned. If you dare...*

Lost

by Amannda G. Maphies

My oldest son, Liam, had basketball practice in the nearby town of Republic, Missouri at 6:30 p.m. on a Monday evening. He rarely practices in Republic, and while I have been to the one gym where his team practices, he assured me this particular night's practice was at an alternate location. One I had *not* been...

Easy peasy...I clicked on the address in the text message from the coach. It took me straight to the spot. Only there was no gym, no church, no outdoor court, no nothing. I literally sat, in our smallish black Rogue SUV, staring at an abandoned intersection on the outskirts of Republic, Missouri, looking confusedly at my phone, which mockingly read, *"You have arrived at your destination."*

Thinking better of dropping my kid off in the middle of nowhere, with creepy looking abandoned warehouses all around, I plugged the address in again ... *and again.* Three times we drove around downtown Republic, for a period of at least half an hour, if not more. Seeing the same sights, looking like we were casing the downtown shops, with me growing increasingly frustrated, while my two sons in the backseat seemed to take great pleasure in my confusion, finding my reaction quite...*comical.*

Finally, I took a closer look at the directions originally sent. There was only one thing missing, *a street address.* Had I read the coach's text in detail in the first place, I could have saved myself a ton of needless trouble, not to mention time! Once the coach clarified the actual *street address* of the gym, we arrived in less than three minutes, and guess what? It was *not* the alternate location my son assured me it was. It was the same location I had taken him before!

So basically, I drove around, in the dark, with my children in tow, looking for a location I already knew how to find, only I didn't know I knew how to find the location...without directions, which it turns out I didn't really need. *How bizarre!*

Are there ever times in life we search diligently for an answer, knowing deep down, in our heart of hearts, the answer has been there all along? Take Dorothy in the epic movie, *The Wizard of Oz*. She knew there was *"No place like home"* all along, yet it was not until someone she thought possessed great power, told her it was okay to go back home, that she actually did find the ability within herself to return from her adventurous and coming-of-age vivid dream in *Oz*. It's probably a good thing Dorothy did not have a smart phone with maps enabled, she might still be aimlessly wondering around the black-and-white version of *Oz*.

I had to laugh at myself for feeling such a hopeless and fearful plight of being lost, when the actual destination was one I had been countless times before. However, those panic-stricken moments, racing against the clock so my son wouldn't be late, wondering where on earth I was and why my GPS was not working, and if I would even make it out of this debacle alive, were quite intense.

"Haunted House on Palmer Drive"

Tales from the young, infamous, blonde duo, Manndi and Emily
by Emily Kelso

The night was cold and dark. The year unknown, but looking back, it must have been around 1993 or so. The season was fall. The month was October. On a glorious Friday evening after school, the long-awaited weekend had finally arrived, and two young friends with plans of a Friday night sleepover were eager to get the fun started.

These girls longed for fun, adventure, laughs, and giggles. They spent time together doing scary things like Snipe hunting in the eerie darkness outside a church lock-in, or walking in the dark graveyard near Manndi's home. It was not unheard of for this dubious pair of blondes to be stuck outside, in inclement weather, while on their random adventures. One such time, they found themselves in the midst of a tornado, while running through the scary maze of graveyard headstones, and trying desperately to get back to the safety of Manndi's house.

Once they were old enough to drive, they would spend many late evenings driving around the country roads outside their small town, and would suddenly scream, or act mystifyingly spooked, just to scare the other unsuspecting girl sitting in the passenger seat. These girls longed for fun and adventure. They found most things in life to be…*hilarious.*

On this particular night in October, just barely teenagers, with driver's licenses being a distant future dream, the dynamic duo agreed that the evening plans at Emily's childhood home would include *the* scariest movie ever known to man (or so believed by these girls), along with popcorn, soda, and homemade tacos.

Bellies full of tacos, a never-ending bowl of popcorn, two full glasses of soda, blankets and pillows laid in the floor to make the comfiest shelter available for refuge from *the* scariest movie ever known to man, and of course, lights out, revealing the pitch blackness of the living room. The girls laid in the center of the floor, fairly close to the television (it was the 90's and televisions were modest in size compared to the large screens of today). They retrieved the VHS tape and realized the last person to watch the movie failed to rewind it. *Irritating*, but at least the VCR was capable of rewinding. VCRs were precious machines you treated with tender, loving care to ensure a long life-span (for any millennials who may be reading this account and have no clue what a VCR is).

Once the movie was rewound, begging to be played, in efforts of spreading fear, adventure, jumps, and screams to the two highly sugared-up little girls, they excitedly hit *Play*.

The obvious movie choice for any spooky, dark, October evening, for adventure and thrill seekers, was none other than…*drumroll*…"***THE HOUSE ON HAUNTED HILL.***" The 1959 classic black and white film, starring Vincent Price. I am sure the girls had a giggle since they had a buddy in school named Vincent, in which they associated the somewhat unique name. Once the giggles were over, the true horror of the movie began.

As the large doors of the mansion creaked open on the screen, the Haunted House was filled with screams. The screen showcased an eerie, looming, dark view of the mansion, coupled with a hologram of the film maker, Vincent Price, which flashed on the screen, hauntingly explaining what was about to happen in the movie, and successfully setting these young, innocent, giggly girls up for a thrill like none other.

An hour or so into the movie, the girls were watching intently, biting their fingernails in between popcorn bites and drinks of soda. The blankets were now over their heads for shelter and on occasion, covering their eyes. Any noise or sudden movement was enough to make them jump. A loud sound…*was that Thunder?* No…it was just a door being shut at the other end of the house. A movement in the window…*WHO'S THERE!?!?* It was just a tree swaying in the chilly wind blowing outside.

I hesitate to reveal any of the spooky, yet enticingly wonderful details of the movie, but I can tell you one of the scenes includes an elderly lady, obviously frightened, and being backed into a corner. She was being chased by, none other than a skeleton, who was slowly, but ever so surely, gaining advancement upon her. She had nowhere to go, running was out of the question. What was she to do in this moment? She stared at the skeleton as he creeped slowly toward her, while backing up to the wall and screaming as loud as she could with her hands held up, helplessly curled in fearful defense.

Manndi and Emily's eyes widened like saucers of terror, glued to the screen, unable to look away from the imminent demise of this poor woman. They were both spooked, senses heightened and dangerously on edge. At least they were in the shelter of the dark living room under the blankets, where they *thought* they were safe. As the skeleton slowly crept toward the old lady in black and white terror, they each grabbed a handful of popcorn, just as the skeleton made contact with his victim.

All of the sudden, the skeleton was not just on the screen, HE WAS IN THE ROOM WITH THEM! THERE WAS SOMEONE STANDING RIGHT BEHIND THEM! They could sense the terrifying presence and feel the warm breath *(do skeletons breathe?)* filling the dark living room. HE WAS THERE … OUT TO GET THEM! They screamed and threw popcorn and jumped completely under the blankets to hide themselves from the menacing evil standing just behind them.

Seconds later (that felt like years due to the sheer terror felt by these two young girls), a lamp mysteriously turned on. The girls slowly peeked out from the blankets to see why the skeleton needed to see. Instead of a skeleton, they saw a silly little blonde-haired boy, laughing hysterically and pointing his bony finger at them. It happened to be Emily's little brother, Jonathan, trying to scare his older sister and her best friend. His prideful face displayed an ecstatic look since he had succeeded. *Job. Well. Done.*

At least they still had some popcorn left and were safe from the skeleton. They finished the movie, enjoying every last morsel of popcorn and sugary drop of soda. Of course, after nearly wetting their pants when Emily's younger brother made his horrifying skeletal appearance, they decided to keep the lamp on. *Just in case.*

I Feel Like...

by Amannda G. Maphies

I have a habit of saying "I feel like..." and then proceeding to document some weird, uncommon, out of the ordinary desire that, in my mind, should be seen as pure, unequivocal *fact*. This is a habit I started years ago, but nonetheless has stuck, and those who know me know when I start off a sentence, "*I feel like...*" there is likely something earth-shattering (and epically ridiculous) about to come out of my mouth.

In today's episode of "*I Feel Like...*" I would like to tackle the idea of cemeteries for fall photo shoots. Allow me to explain...

I drive by the most beautiful, scenic, picturesque cemetery on my way to work every morning. I should also mention it is mid-November in Missouri, so we are experiencing the peak of Maple leaf color changing season. The trees are simply magnificent. The vivid reds, oranges, yellows... it is truly breathtaking. A vibrant sight to behold. Sure, you see a random tree resembling this autumnal beauty every now and then. But to see *so* many of them in one place at one time is just *out of the world* spectacular.

Which leads me to my idea...why not utilize the cemetery for photo shoots? Tis the season for Christmas pictures, holiday cards, senior pictures, baby pictures, engagement pictures, even wedding pictures. Now I am not a complete hobo here. I do not think sitting on a gravestone and snapping selfies would be appropriate. I am talking about taking advantage of the peaceful atmosphere and colorful beauty to snap some incredible shots to brighten one's living room, feature one's holiday card, occupy a Facebook profile, or treasured cover photo.

There are likely places in the cemetery where a photo opportunity can be gained without viewing the large monuments, stone angel statues, or crumbling headstones in the background. Even if you get a hint of these historically beautiful pillars, is that really such a bad thing? Some of the most beautiful statues I have ever witnessed have been found in local cemeteries.

There is a cemetery we visit every year at Memorial Day, where my grandparents are buried. On the way to their gravesites, we pass the sweetest little lamb etched in stone and marking the grave of a young child. It makes me sad each time I see it, for obvious reasons. But I also love the beautiful simplicity and peaceful sense you get from seeing the baby lamb guarding the precious child whose time on earth was cut tragically short.

Another plus to taking pictures in cemeteries is that you could quite possibly end up with a ghostly spiritual orb in your photos! While some may be distraught at such an added bonus, others (*like me*) would find it entertaining and extremely note-worthy. Professional photos are expensive, people. Why not get more bang (*or Boo's*) for your buck? Not to mention a memorable photo sure to be a conversation piece for years to come. It may even prompt you to do some research on the local cemetery in an attempt to find out who mysteriously made their presence known and what story they may have to tell. *Key the Twilight Zone music...*

Whether or not you agree with my assessment of local cemeteries as the perfect photographic backdrop, I hope I have given you some thoughts to consider. Imagine your local family cemetery as the setting for all of your momentous photo shoots and someday in the distant future, your very own children and children's children may be apt to use that same locale for the same purpose.

Perhaps you will even find a way to *visit* and be part of the family legacy photo shoot, taking the prime opportunity to *check in* on your loved ones and say *Hello* ...

Dating a Vampire

by Amannda G. Maphies

And now it all makes perfect sense. As much sense as dating, starting to fall in love with, and being dumped by a vampire can possibly make…

The just-shy-of-four-week-love-affair that was my relationship with Vladamir (name changed to protect the not-so-innocent) is now a…..*closed chapter*. It ended with his final words: "I'm just not feeling it." I was feeling something in that moment (something strangely akin to a violent desire to rip his face off and feed it to a freshly-awakened, starved mother grizzly in the midst of deep hibernation season).

However, I kept it to myself, gave him a hug, ignored his underwhelming and inauthentic plea for my wellbeing and drove straight home. This was the first break-up (which is ironic since we were never officially *together*) in which I refused to waste one single tear. As Johnny Castle in "Dirty Dancing" emphatically tells Robby the waiter/man-whore who knocked Penny up and then lied about it: "You're not worth it!"

Still, I have never had someone occupy such a large presence in my life, only to disappear into some dark mysterious abyss as if he never actually existed. If it were not for the randomly impersonal texts followed by the even more random, even less personal Facebook messages, I would question if he ever existed in the first place. Those seldom (now pretty much non-existent) likes on Facebook are the only evidence I have of the man I thought for a fleeting second was *the one.*

Turns out, he was *the one. The one* that seemingly fell in love with me one day, only to carelessly toss me into the infinite black hole of jilted lovers the next. Oh sure, he was *the one* alright. *The one* asshole I waited my whole life to find, only to wish he had stayed buried in his deep, dark, abysmal pit of narcissistic, torturous prison.

Fast-forward a couple of weeks. Still completely shell-shocked and wondering what happened, but resigned to, "it's insignificant enough that I should not care (though hating myself for actually caring)", I start reading a book called "Inception: A Dark Paranormal Romance." Yes, it is a love story...about vampires. No, I will not apologize for my immature millennial obsession that started with the "Twilight" series, morphed into "Vampire Diaries" followed by "Buffy The Vampire Slayer," "Interview with a Vampire," "Dracula" and all other movies, shows, and Netflix encounters vampire-related.

Torn between her love of two men (pretty sure one, or possibly both, is a vampire), the sweet, innocent, clumsily adorable main character loquaciously describes her otherworldly forbidden romance in words that ring loud and clear: dark, brooding, emotionally unattached, keeps people at a distance, cold, mysterious, tendency toward violence, seemingly allergic to light of any kind (artificial or sunlight) black soul. In a mere 26 words, I have perfectly described the personality of *Vladamir*. Yes, folks. He is a vampire. *And I dated him.*

I suppose I should be thankful he did not see fit to violently slay me and drink my blood, turning me into an immortally evil shadowy being of the night. It really is no mystery as to why he had an attraction to me. I am everything he is not: light, cheery, endearing, deep, chipper, soulful, beautiful, intuitive...you get the point. Perhaps it was the forbidden romance equation. He loved me so deeply and so desperately that he could not bear the thought of reconstructing my beautiful human *mortal* soul with that of a dark, macabre, evil, insidiously *immortal* one.

'Tis best to live a short life of love and light than a long life of hate and night.

Yah, we'll go with that. Much easier to accept than the alternative: *He just wasn't that into me.*

In light of this unfortunate experience, I thought it would be useful to include my newfound knowledge to help others avoid falling into the pit of despair the way I so naively did. We as women must unite and save ourselves from these evil man-posing *demons of disguise.*

If you happen to meet a tall, dark, mysterious stranger at a late-night bar and he is showing all signs of being *into you*, yet makes no effort to contact you within a day (or three) for a meeting during *daylight* hours, he *might* be a vampire.

Remember, all men look fabulously tasty late at night (especially after a few drinks when wearing the ever-deceptive wine glasses). Reserve proper judgment for when (rather *if*) you see him during daylight hours.

If the man you meet often wears a long, black, out-of-style trench coat (think John Bender in *The Breakfast Club*), he is *quite possibly* a vampire.

Looking back (rather *Facebook stalking*), I noticed he went through a fashion phase that could only be appreciated by the dark underworld drug lords that cease to exist in the shining light of day. Thus, if his fashion isn't *forward*, leave him in the past with his out-of-style threads in tow.

If he invites you to his castle, beckoning you into a foreboding, creepy, run-down home, he is *very likely* a vampire. I still get shivers thinking of his *Addams Family-esque* house and how it gave *Netflix and chill* a whole new meaning.

If the chap loves dark comedies (*Slingblade*, *Tombstone* or *Deadwood*) and seemingly has every line of the movie memorized, reciting it perfectly and expecting you to be exceptionally impressed by his acting abilities (or *lack* thereof), it is *highly probable* he is a vampire.

If your man disappears for long, inexplicable absences without texting, calling or dropping by, then shows up unannounced with no rhyme or reason, he is *undeniably* a vampire. What the hell was he doing for three days straight with no contact? Camping in the Grand Canyon? Hiking the Serengeti? Taking in a Vegas show? Then showing up in the highest spirits like he has just partied like a rock star (or perhaps feasted on human flesh with a glass of dry red chianti (aka *blood)*, Vintage 1820). No thank you! *I'll pass...*

If your boy toy has 2500 friends on Facebook; 2499 are female; and it appears he has dated 2498 of them, he is *most likely* a special version of a vampire known as a *Manpire Vamp*. (Basically a male whore that sucks blood; targeting young beautiful women in an attempt to seduce them and viciously deplete them of their humanity, turning them into shadowy, immortal beings with no soul and a penchant for darkness, devastation, and death).

If your gent is a former cop, fireman, security guard or other service industry operative with heavy emphasis on brooding mysterious looks and vain egotistical traits, he is *absolutely, positively, undeniably* 100% VAMPIRE!

You may be fortunate to escape his sinister and sultry taste of death. However, you will *not* come out unscathed. *If* you suspect you are dealing with a vampire, do yourself a favor and run as far and as fast as you can in the opposite direction, never once looking back.

*This story previously appeared in The Syndrome Magazine. You can find the original version at:
https://thesyndromemag.com/dating-a-vampire-a-guide-for-millennials/

Don't Say My Name!

by Amannda G. Maphies

IF being scared out of your wits is on your bucket list (possibly the very last item before the inevitable end), I highly recommend the Haunted House at the *Lemp Brewery* in downtown St. Louis, Missouri.

For the low price of $25/person ($20 if you are a Groupon guru like me), you can have mysterious monsters jump out at you from dark corners, weirdos with chainsaws stare you down while revving their chain-less engine, *Ratman* warning you of a severe rat infestation ahead, strobe lights making you feel like you are sky high on a very bad morel mushroom, pitch blackness with the stranger behind you grabbing your arm (Oh Wait. *I* was the stranger grabbing the poor gal in front of me), psyhco clowns creepily saying your name (*How did they know my name?!*), and a zombie literally chasing you out of the brewery at top speed, blowing in your hair and making kissing noises.

I seriously cannot make this stuff up. These are merely the parts that I remember. I think I briefly passed out for 15-20 minutes of the *fun* due to sheer fright. *And my date.* That precious dude was no help whatsoever! (I think he may have actually *encouraged* the monsters, goat-demons, zombies, and witches to torture me, grossly adding to his own brand of demented entertainment).

If all of this seems like your *thing*, by all means…*Go for It!* As for me, I now look 73 years old and every muscle in my body hurts from tensing every time I rounded a corner.

Dr. Phil suggests immersion therapy to overcome fears. I say *BS*! Never again, Dr. Phil…*NEVER AGAIN!*

Madman in the Cemetery

by Amannda G. Maphies

Years ago…many, many, *many* years ago, I was a runner. This was during my high school/college days. One dismal cloudy fall afternoon, I decided to jog toward the cemetery down the road from where I lived. I never minded running in the cemetery. In fact, I rather enjoyed the quiet tranquility and lack of traffic. It was a rather large cemetery for my small hometown, which meant less laps than the local track.

On this particular day, I set out around 4:00 p.m. Being late autumn, I did not have much daytime left. As I was mindlessly running around the cemetery, I noticed a shadowed vision of a man out of the corner of my eye. The man was just entering the cemetery and wearing a stocking cap so I could not make out the details of his face. I assumed he was just a neighbor out for a leisurely evening walk.

As I continued my run, the sky got darker by the second. The man appeared to be getting closer to the route I was taking. I started getting a bit anxious, as I was taught from a young age, to always be aware of my surroundings … especially in the dark, and in a *cemetery!*

The more distance I tried to put between me and the mystery man in the cemetery, the more he seemed intent on closing the gap between us. I started to get concerned. It felt as if this strange man was attempting to give me a message … *or kill me*. I wasn't sure which. But I can still feel the fear coursing through my veins as I recall that incident from my youth.

The more the man lined his path closer to mine, the faster I ran. At this point, I was running a steady race-pace when I had started at just a comfortable jog. I tried to formulate a plan to exit the cemetery and get back to my house. The only problem was, there was only one way out of the cemetery, and the man in darkness was blocking the entrance/exit, leaving me a prisoner running continuous laps amongst the dark tombstones surrounding me.

I tried to throw the man off by heading one direction, putting as much space between us as I could manage, then quickly turning and sprinting the opposite direction, making a beeline for the exit. At this point, my lungs were burning, my legs were cramping, and my heart was beating strongly from a combination of fear, panic, and the rhythmic beating of push-it-to-the-limit-aerobic exertion. I was also praying I could manage to escape the man I was certain, at that point, was trying to kill me.

I ran as fast as my little high school legs would carry me. I made it to the entrance of the cemetery and sprinted down the hill, turned right, and ran with all my might to my driveway, through the yard, and practically fell flat on my face when I entered the kitchen of my home. I did not allow myself to look backward on my full sprint to my house, I needed all the momentum I could muster to avoid the certain near-death I was trying desperately to escape.

As I breathlessly entered my house, I found my mother in the kitchen fixing dinner. My Dad was nowhere in sight. I started retelling my account of the near murderous scene in the cemetery. My mother looked...amused, entertained even. I swore she had a half-smile plastered to her face, which I found very disconcerting, considering I just told her of my most recent near-death experience!

A few minutes later, after finally catching my breath and allowing the adrenaline to leave my body, the kitchen door opened. In walked my dad...wearing the exact same clothing and stocking cap as the murderer in the cemetery. Wait...*what*?! How could this be?

With a half-smile on his face and a twinkle of humor in his eyes, he said, *"Well, Manndi... I have never seen you run that fast!"* Recognition dawned in my mind as I realized it was my own father in the cemetery! He was worried about me running in the dark and my mom told him to walk to the cemetery and keep an eye on me. Of course, I felt like the biggest idiot in the world.

Fortunately, the only witnesses to this bizarre scene were my dad, myself, and a cemetery full of dead folks, who I am quite sure, would have greatly enjoyed the harrowing game of cat and mouse, only one of us failed to realize was meant to keep me safe!

Lucky Day

by Amannda G. Maphies

Lightening doesn't strike twice;
Thunder is on the horizon.
Watch out for that crack, son,
Your momma won't survive it.

Third time is a charm;
I'm waiting for a break.
Please throw me some rope, Lord,
How much more can I take?

That ladder is in my way;
Just crossed paths with a black cat.
I can't take any more bad luck,
Damn this cowboy's hat!

I am going to head for the hills;
Look for signs in the trees.
Outrun this bad luck,
Fall down on my knees.

Lord, I can't take anymore!
What do you want me to see?
Just speak to me, Father…
Help me to believe.

My faith has been tested;
I have refused to give in.
Please throw me a life raft,
Until I can find the strength to swim.

Horseshoes and ladders,
Mean nothing to me.
My faith is in you, God.
My trusty anchor at sea.

This four-leaf clover,
Won't do a thing for me.
My luck is not bound,
By earthly pedigree.

I vow to rise above,
I commit to finish strong.
No lucky number seven,
Will break this sailor's song.

One day I will look back,
And recall, with a hint of a smile.
This bump in the road,
This never-ending uphill mile.

I will think it all through;
With a grateful and humble heart.
And know beyond a shadow of doubt,
He gracefully provided strength for each new start.

Chapter 5

Animal Encounters and Messages from Beyond

Meow….

Hamilton, the Black Cat

by Amannda G. Maphies

There is a black cat named Hamilton;
Frightened of his own shadow is he.
Yet always up for adventure;
Falling steadfast into his curiosity.

This black cat was born on Halloween;
He was as tiny as a new baby bird.
We waited until he was ready;
And adopted him in January 2018.

At first, he was timid and fearful;
Then he became used to the chaos of his new home.
He was loved from the very first day;
No lack of attention for this tiny ball of black fur.

He developed a personality all his own;
With a special bond with my youngest son, Waylan.
Hammie and Waylan were inseparable;
Still the best of friends to this day.

It has been said black cats are bad luck;
Spooky souls come to haunt and cause trouble.
That is the furthest from truth with our Hammie;
Who is afraid of his very own shadow.

He is a typical cat, of course;
Assuming he owns our whole home.
And runs the occupants within these four walls;
Like a judge sitting upon his fated thrown.

Always up for a nap and a cuddle;
He lies in wait for me to get in my favorite chair.
Then slowly he crouches near and climbs up onto my lap;
Kneading his paws here, there, and everywhere.

He barely meows unless he is hungry;
He made friends with the two dogs in our home.
He enjoys peaceful days with the house to himself;
But seems excited when his people return home.

Are black cats scary or evil?
Not in the least I would say.
Our Hamilton Jennings is quite the opposite;
An angel of black with shining eyes of pure gold.

The Magic of Cats

by Amannda G. Maphies

Waylan is my youngest son. If you know of, or have met Waylan, you most likely know about Hamilton. Hamilton is our black cat. We adopted him from the local Humane Society almost four years ago. He was supposed to be a Christmas gift for my two sons but was not quite ready to go home by Christmas, so he was more of a New Year's gift.

Waylan has always had an affinity for cats. But when Hamilton came along, his previous love of felines grew exponentially. He and Hamilton (Hammie) were inseparable. Waylan talked to him like a child, cuddled him like a baby, and played with him like a brother. It was adorable.

Now Hamilton has grown out of the kitten phase and settled contently into the less playful yet still curious young adult phase. He spends his days lazily migrating from room to room, with a fresh desire to nap in a different location every few hours. His energetic time is, of course, 3:00 in the morning, when he finds it hilarious to perch at the end of my bed and wait diligently for me to shift positions so he can attack my feet. Hamilton is not declawed. My comforter is not thick. You do the math.

I love Hamilton. I wanted a jet-black cat from the time I was a little girl and read the stories about Dorrie and her beloved cat, Gink. I pictured myself as a young wayward witch with her trusty black cat at her heels, just as Gink followed Dorrie and loyally engaged in her outlandish magical adventures.

Hammie arrived when I was in my late 30s. I had outgrown the pretend magical witch phase, but I was still drawn to black cats. Sometimes, late at night, something will startle me awake and I will peer beyond my bedroom into the hallway. I will see this black shadow sitting there with yellow eyes glowing through the darkness. It was a bit unsettling the first time I saw this vision, but now that I know it is Hammie, performing his nightly prowl, it comforts me to know that one member of our household is on protective watch as the rest of us sleep soundly.

Hammie often finds his way to Waylan's bedroom at night. Waylan has a top bunk with storage underneath. How Hamilton is able to locate himself on the top bunk, I do not know. But Waylan is delighted anytime Hammie chooses to spend time with him.

This morning, after Waylan's morning chores, he came into my room and got in bed with me for the last three snooze sessions before I forced myself to get up and around. As I laid there, still partially asleep, Waylan began a conversation about his beloved cat. His best friend.

He told me about Hamilton sleeping in his bed. He further explained that sometimes Hamilton simply stares at him. Deep into his eyes. "Mom, it's like he can see though to my soul." This, from a 9-year-old. (Can you tell his mother is a creative writer?)

Years ago, I had a cat named Zeke. My then-husband and I got her and her sister, Zoie, as kittens from the same litter. About six months after bringing them home, Zeke was traumatically hit by a vehicle on the road near where we lived. We never found poor Zoie. I wonder, to this day, what happened to her and hope that some nice, loving family gave her a welcome and loving home.

There was one time when we lived in Columbia, MO. I was going through a difficult adjustment period and feeling very depressed and lonely. I recall lying on the couch late one night, while my husband was upstairs studying. Zeke jumped up to the couch and perched herself inches from my face. She looked deeply into my eyes. I literally felt hypnotized by her intense stare. I stayed in the trance for several minutes. I am not sure what broke the magical spell she put on me, but it was a strange and somewhat otherworldly occurrence, which I have never forgotten.

When Waylan told me Hammie often does this with him, *stares into his soul*, it automatically jolted me back to a time and place when Zeke hypnotized me with her unique cat magic.

Truth be told, I am more of a dog person. I love that my dogs are loyal, obedient (sometimes), and needy of my attention. Hammie is the typical cat. He wants attention on his terms, he is a bit judgy and entitled, and seems to think we are living in *his* house.

That being said, I do believe cats possess some form of mystical magic. Their eyes are beautifully captivating. Their movements are nothing short of years of obediently trained gymnastic poise. They are so confident and assured. Yet, can become easily spooked by nothing more than a slight sound or whisper of the wind. I often wonder if they have the ability to see things humans are not capable of seeing.

When Waylan told me Hammie stared deep into his eyes and entranced him in a spell, I was not surprised in the least. Cats have that power. I do not believe it is a wicked or evil power. I believe it is simply the magic God implanted into their DNA. Cats are curious creatures by nature. Yet, the humans who love them are often more intrigued by their spiritual presence than we can adequately explain. I know my curiosity is piqued by the head-shaking bizarre things Hammie does. He definitely keeps his people entertained. And while we sometimes have to beg for it, his attention is undeniably desired.

Angel Cat with a Touching Message

by Felicia Evelyn Morales

I saw a shadow. I slowly went to investigate what was outside. Turns out, it was just my backyard buddy visiting …

For those who do not know, and even those who *do*, long story short, my brother had a female cat that looked just like this one when we were kids. Her name was *Peaches*. I remember her sleeping with him every night.

My brother passed away 12 years ago. He was my best friend. My big brother. About 2 years ago, I began to notice a fairly frequent visitor in my backyard. I have 2 decks. The local feral cats roam my bottom deck often, doing anything to avoid my 2 beagles. None of these nightly visitors have ever advanced to the top deck. They know better.

But not this girl. *She is brave.* She comes up when she sees me in my room. She sits and waits for me. She is my comfort. She makes me feel like Bobby is with me. And no, I cannot take her in, as she is feral and definitely would not be happy away from her natural habitat. She is meant for the outdoors.

My son is highly allergic to cats, and I have 2 beagles that are not huge cat fans. Thus, this beauty lives in the backyard behind me, where the cat lady has been sheltering and feeding the local wild cats for years.

I believe this sweetheart appears to me when my brother senses I need him. Or…when she wants to be fed. She will not allow me to touch her. But she sits on the deck until I go to bed. I watch her on my camera. When she sees my television go off, she leaves.

Thank you, Bobby…for my Angel.
My reminder that you are always here.

Yansi

by Amannda G. Maphies

As a young child, for as long as I could remember, I wanted a cat. My parents repeatedly and emphatically told me *No* since we lived in town, and they did not want to see my little girl heart broken when a cat either ran away or was viciously run over in front of my little girl baby blue eyes.

I never gave up my dream of having a cat and I must have finally worn my parents down. We had a couple at our hometown church who had barn kittens and agreed to give us one right around Christmastime, unbeknownst to my little girl self.

I can still see my parents walking into the living room of my childhood home. Holding a pale blue animal carrier (which I still have nearly thirty years later) with the face of a little orange tabby kitten curiously peeking out at me from inside. My heart was absolutely delighted! I was in love with this kitten at first sight. We ravished the baby name book my mom kept from when she was expecting me, in hopes of picking out the perfect name for our furry new family member. The name we chose was, *Yansi* (meaning: An Englishman with Yorkshire descent). It was a strong and noble name for such a tiny creature, but we had no doubt he would eventually grow into it.

Yansi grew to be a gentle and patient tom cat. I shamelessly dressed him in my baby clothes and attempted to walk him on a leash. I can picture the neighbors watching *Little Manndi* with her cat, Yansi, on his green leash, dragging him down the street since he literally sat down and refused to walk.

Yansi disappeared at one point and, after about five days with no sign of my feline friend, my parents feared the worst. I had not given up my little girl hope that Yansi would eventually find his way home as his disappearances were somewhat frequent, but never this long at a time.

Late one summer night, with my bedroom windows open and a

gentle breeze blowing on my face, I laid in bed and earnestly prayed for Yansi's miraculous return. I happened to hear the tinkling of a bell in the distance. *Could it be?!* I jumped out of bed and excitedly ran to our back patio, the direction in which I heard the bell.

There, in the flesh, was a starved looking Yansi, wearing his little green collar with the bell I had heard moments before. *Yansi had come home!* I later learned that my neighbor, who traveled for weeks at a time, had also come home that night. We assumed Yansi had been locked up in his garage for the time he was away. However, my childlike mind, full of faith and hope, believed fervently this was a miracle straight from Heaven above.

Yansi was the first of many cats I have owned (or rather, *owned me*). Yet, there is something special about a child's first pet. He was not my first pet, but he was my first cat, and I never formed a bond quite like the childhood bond I had with Yansi. For being a cat, he was less snobbish, judgy, selfish and narcissistic than any cat I have known since! Seeing my nine-year-old son, Waylan, with his beloved black cat, Hamilton (Hammie), heartwarmingly reminds me of *Little Manndi* with her precious orange tabby, *Yansi*. Kindred spirits and best of friends. Evidence that cats really do seem to have (at least) nine lives...

A Star is Born...

Atlas Orion Wilkins

by Amannda G. Maphies

Orion is a star shining bright;
Strategically perched against the black of night.
A whisper from Heaven to loved ones below;
A dream a granddaughter would soon come to know.

Years in the making;
She had this vivid dream.
To name a sweet baby…
"Orion," it seemed.

I mindlessly mocked her plan;
Choosing other, less-unique names.
Yet a gnawing sensation ate at my soul;
A dream to fulfil, a promise to extol.

I vowed once upon a time;
To gift a loved one with this name.
A spiritual connection so strong;
A desire previously untamed.

This new and welcome life;
This precious puppy boy.
How chosen he should feel;
To don this sacred title.

His spark and zest for life;
Undefined by his small size.
His name alone encapsulates a star shown;
Against every blackened cloudless sky.

Atlas may be young and petite;
A trait shared by Joann Dolores Mann.
Yet his passion is sure to run deep;
A true warrior of both sky and land.

Truly loved is this baby boy;
This tiny ball of fur.
Atlas Orion Wilkins, he shall be!
Inspired by a dream…a namesake just for her.

Orion

by Amannda G. Maphies

I have authored many writings about my dear grandmother, Joann Dolores Mann Wadlow. She is not only my namesake (the very person responsible for the *uniquely* confounding spelling of my name), but she was and *is* one of the most inspiring women I have ever known. She did not inspire in the traditional sense. Rather, her inspiration came from the way she lived, the way she made her own rules, marching to the beat of her own drum and embracing her *differences* as God's masterful vision of the before her time, outspoken, often witty, always fashionable, at times political, immeasurably crafty, precious tiny little woman with the biggest personality ever.

My grandmother was quirky, opinionated, could be sweet as pie one minute and vicious as a mama grizzly the next. She admired my outrageous imagination as a child. She laughed at my awkward attempts to be funny (she was often the only one). She once told me, "You say the strangest things! And mostly, you're very funny!" Ironically, she never fully understood me, but ours was a relationship that surpassed understanding. We were similar soul creatures who enjoyed the simple pleasures in life.

My grandma taught me to celebrate my unique spirit and never, ever conform to the masses. My family often joked about her love for random, unique, and at times, oddball names. When I was expecting my first son, my grandma (very seriously) suggested *Elspeth* for a girl and *Orion* for a boy. After I stopped laughing because I thought she was kidding (she was *not* kidding), I kindly told her I preferred something a little less…*strange*. In her typical *you are not as smart as you think you are* look, she said her usual snarky-infused, nose-upturned, "*Okay,*" and moved on.

I once saw a Silpada piece of jewelry titled *Orion*. I knew when I saw the name of the ring, I had to have it. After a quick search on google, I discovered Orion is the brightest, most outstanding and recognizable constellation in the sky. In addition, it has been referred to as *angel's breath against a frosted sky*. Very fitting for a piece of jewelry reminding me of my precious grandmother. Not only was she outstanding on earth, but she continues to shine her light on me from Heaven above. Yesterday, today, always, and forever.

Someday, I vow to name something or someone...*Orion*.

Pondering the Infinite Beyond that Which We Know

by Amannda G. Maphies

The one nice thing about having to take the puppy-child out in freezing cold temps late at night is that I get to do a bit of stargazing. I have always loved a jet-black sky with glimmers of light and the occasional shooting star painting a picture overhead. The sheer beauty and intrigue that comes with wondering what lies beyond the known of our small human minds.

I believe in Heaven. If there is a Heaven, there is undoubtedly a Hell, so I believe in that too, though I do not care to fantasize about a place of torturous abandonment. Heaven, however, I could romanticize all day long (or night, as the case may be).

Is the Heaven that lies outside our earthly realm painted with the majestic mountains I so adore here upon this earth, the glittering lights of stars above, the rushing waters of a river wild, the vast fields and rolling hills that bring comfort and reminiscent memories of a simpler time and place?

Are the streets of gold really paths of smoothly polished pebbles leading the way to that hilltop mansion mentioned in the familiar hymns I sang as a child? Is the glowing sun shrouded by clouds to cast rays of laser light upon the distant hills? Or an afternoon shower followed by the brilliant colors of a rainbow spanning the sky when the sun displays its glorious light...

Will my beloved pets come running...ears flopping in the gentle wind and licking my face with delight at a long-overdue reunion? Will my loved ones follow suit and welcome me home with the hospitality of angels lying in wait for new recruits? Will Jesus reach out to gently touch my hand or embrace me in a bear hug to rival the warmest, most comforting mecca of love felt upon this earth? Will my senses be heightened, experiencing an ecstasy of pleasant smell, soft touch, beautiful music, glorious views, and mouth-watering tastes?

How small I feel when standing in my backyard, peering up at a darkened midnight sky and expectantly gazing to find a familiar pattern of stars. The order of the universe. The vast space which lies beyond human comprehension. The beauty we know, allowing us to wonder how Heaven could possibly be more enchanting than the few places left upon this earth remaining innocently untapped by human hands.

All musings of my weary mind while waiting for Atlas Orion, my newly adopted cockapoo puppy, to take his final nightly pee. Life is beautiful. God is most certainly present in the magical details, giving but a small glimmer of the glorious pleasure yet to come...

The Missing Black Dog

by Amannda G. Maphies

Early this morning, I opened the back door to let the dogs in before I left for work. Lucy loyally greeted me at the door and went straight to her kennel, as she does every morning. Atlas was nowhere to be found. He usually stands at the backdoor and waits to be let in. Not to mention he does not let Lucy out of his sight when they are outside. For him to not come when I called was odd.

After the third time calling his name, I started freaking out. Thinking he had escaped the backyard, been kidnapped (or is it dog-napped?), the victim of a vicious owl attack, my mind was reeling with the endless terrifying possibilities. The more I called his name, the more concerned I got that something terrible had happened to my favorite little cockapoo.

Finally, thinking I would go in search of the little bugger, I shut the back door and walked into the kitchen to lock Lucy's crate. As I walked by Atlas' crate, there he was...in all his black glory, eating his breakfast, with not a care in the world. Apparently, in the chilling dark of this autumn morning, he snuck right by me and landed in his crate while I was furiously calling his name in the backyard, my fear (and level of shouting) increasing with each passing moment.

I yelled at him. Then realized he did not do anything wrong. I apologized. He paid no attention to either, as he was happily eating his morning kibble. How many other things, people, experiences, shadows, ghosts, spirits, angels, you-name-it pass right by without me noticing? It is truly a frightening, if not exciting, prospect to ponder ...

To Do Item: Spray paint black dog...*white*.

Misplaced Fears

by Amannda G. Maphies

This morning, I was contemplating safety...*and fear*. This little fluff nugget provides a beautiful illustration of how fear can easily be directed toward unwarranted objects, while real, everyday dangers often go unchecked.

As I was standing in the bathroom early Saturday morning, preparing for the day, I happened to see something out of the corner of my eye which captured my attention. I turned to find my little cockapoo, head deep in the wastebasket, rummaging through the trash, and spreading it all over one side of the room. Atlas has done this countless times and you would have thought I would learn to *put the trashcan up*. But *nooooooo*. It was early. I was tired. Shaking my head and heaving an overly dramatized sigh of annoyance, I grabbed the trashcan, thrust in on the counter, and went in search of the broom to clean up the mass of refuse littering the bathroom floor.

Minutes later, after sweeping up the mess and lightly scolding the wide-eyed little bugger, I went back to my morning routine. As I stood washing my face, I heard a low growl and again, noticed movement out of the corner of my eye. Propped against the wall was the broom and dustpan. Atlas was in full attack mode just feet from the broom. Every few minutes he would lunge forward, then get scared and quickly back up, all while growling at the broom in the corner. I could not help but watch this display for longer than I care to admit. It was hilarious. My sweet little cockapoo was heroically defending me from...*a broom*.

As I replayed this bizarre scenario in my head countless times, I was mentally taken back two weekends prior, when Atlas and his dad, my fiancé, Justin, were on the back patio, starting a fire for the evening. From deep inside the house, I heard the nervous shouts of his name coming from Justin's voice. I ran outside, fearing the worst. Atlas was nowhere to be found. It was pitch black, and without the sound of the bell on his collar alerting us to his whereabouts, there was absolutely no way to see our pitch-black puppy running around in the dangerous darkness and terrorizing shadows of night.

There is a creek behind Justin's house, in front of which is a large field. I had horrific visions of Atlas being attacked by an owl, mauled by a bobcat, violated by a coyote, or simply making his way to the busy highway at the end of the subdivision and, not knowing the fear of cars, getting hit on the roadside, with no one to tend to his brutal wounds. My mind was a flutter of nervous energy. Fearing the worst, while shots of adrenaline rushed through my body, as I ran around the field calling his name with a mixture of desperation, fear, and anger.

After what felt like hours, my little black cockapoo came running from somewhere deep in the woods beyond the house. His little bell jingling in time with his short legs. He practically jumped into my arms. I hugged him tightly...perhaps a little too tightly. I declared my love for this young, tiny, wooly beast. I scolded him. Then I apologized because he does not know any better. He is a dog. It is in his DNA to explore, follow scents, and find adventure. I can't exactly snuff that out of him, nor would I want to. Still, the mutt has no idea the dangers that lie outside his safe and secure surroundings.

How typical is Atlas' behavior (fearing an inanimate object versus running into the dark night full of danger with absolutely no idea what perils lie at his little padded feet) to us as God's children? How many times have I needlessly worried about items of little consequence, while completely ignoring the looming danger at my heels?

We tend to worry about those things God has completely in His control: relationships, careers, health issues, children, where to live, what to drive, which job to take, which school to attend, which outfit to wear. The list of worries stealing sleep each night is endless. All this worry and fear eats away at our psyches. The bigger monsters lie waiting in the darkness, poised and ready for attack, using distraction as their greatest weapon.

The monsters I am referring to are those silent but deadly sins we tend to sweep under the rug. Monsters such as jealousy, anger, bitterness, refusal to forgive, hatred, and greed, to name just a few. I have been guilty of this in my own life. Metaphorically barking at the broom in the corner, when there is a much larger darkness trying desperately to take hold of my spirit.

What better testament to the comfort God provides than that found in, perhaps the most quoted Bible verse, *Psalm 23*:

1 The LORD is my shepherd, I lack nothing. 2 He makes me lie down in green pastures, he leads me beside quiet waters, 3 he refreshes my soul. He guides me along the right paths for his name's sake. 4 Even though I walk through the darkest valley, I will fear no evil, for you are with me; your rod and your staff, they comfort me. 5 You prepare a table before me in the presence of my enemies. You anoint my head with oil; my cup overflows. 6 Surely your goodness and love will follow me all the days of my life, and I will dwell in the house of the LORD forever.

The breath of peace I feel upon reciting these words is astounding. *"The Lord is my shepherd."*

Just as I am Atlas' *shepherd* (with a slightly different fashion sense), I will protect that little soul with all my might. How much more will my heavenly Father protect me from evil, daily lurking in the shadows of my own life? The more in tune we are with Jesus, the more aware of the danger which looms ahead on our daily path. With knowledge, comes the desire to stick close to the one who offers protection against those forces that often sneak up on us with no warning.

His rescue is divine. His care is overwhelming. His comfort is enough. His love is unwavering.

Stick close to the Savior who shepherds His own as if He owns a flock of one.

Whoooooo Goes There?

The Owl Angel that Visited Me

by Amannda G. Maphies

Yesterday, my mother shared a Facebook post about *signs*. As an avid X-Files fan, she adamantly believes *the truth is out there*. More importantly, she believes the truth lies within us all. We just have to *ask, seek, knock* and the door will be open to us.

I have been doing *a lot* of knocking these past four weeks. At times, it feels like no one is on the other side of the door. But just when I feel defeated, unheard, and alone, God will use someone *or something* to speak louder than ever before. He faithfully reminds me that He *is* listening, He *does* care and He *is* working through the pain, loss, and suffering felt by so many after Chuck's seemingly untimely death.

My prayer of late has been that He will speak to me in ways I will understand. This morning, on my way to work, exactly three years since the passing of my grandma and four weeks since the passing of my love, I saw this beautiful owl, looking down on me from his perch on an electrical wire. I will not go into the great (and possibly dangerous) lengths I went to get this picture. But anyone who knows me, knows my love for owls is more of an obsession with the wise and beautiful creatures. My grandma knew it as we both shared the same passion for the winged guardians and Chuck knew it because well, I told him...*constantly*!

He brought me treasures from every trip. Many times, they were unique owls...a wire sculpture from San Francisco, CA, a wooden owl whistle from Vail, CO, a beautifully carved stone owl from Cabo, a Kate Spade owl purse for Valentine's Day, and the list goes on. My point is that Chuck accepted my love for owls. God heard my prayer requesting a sign I would beyond-a-shadow-of-doubt understand. *And Voila!* I get my first ever owl visit on a morning it was desperately needed and overwhelmingly appreciated.

I believe in angels. I also believe they come in many different forms. I honestly do not believe there could be a more serendipitous being destined to guide me than a winged, feathered, beautifully celestial bird I so abundantly adore.

Messenger of the Night

by Amannda G. Maphies

"On a dark desert highway, cool wind in my hair..."

Last night, as we were driving home from good friends' combination birthday party/wedding reception, my fiancé, Justin, pulled up to a stop sign, in the middle of *Nowhere, Missouri*. Sitting atop the sign was an owl. I rolled my window down for a better look. He got spooked and flew into the trees.

As an owl lover and spiritual enthusiast for the nocturnal bird of prey, I hopped out of the truck to try and capture his image on my trusty iPhone camera. Obviously, the pictures turned out very poorly. However, the experience was quite chilling. This particular owl sat on a branch and stared me down for no less than three intense minutes of pure bliss.

Was he carrying a message?

Was he distracting us from danger ahead?

Was he simply out for an early evening snack and we happened upon his chosen fast-food country locale?

Whatever the reason, owls, to me, symbolize wisdom, intrigue, mysterious messages, and mystical delight. I was honored he chose to reveal himself in the dark of night on that deserted country highway in the Ozark Hills of Southwest Missouri.

Perhaps his message will become clear in time. For now, I keep replaying that vividly perfect mind's eye image of seeing him perched mysteriously atop a stop sign, mere feet from our vehicle, staring deeply into my soul.

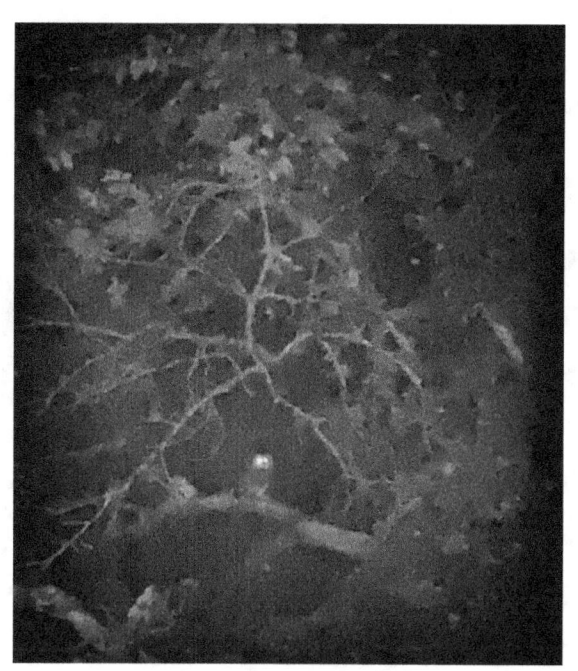

Messages from Beyond...

A Message from Beyond

Wednesday, March 21, 2018
by Amannda G. Maphies

Last night, while out with friends, one of the ladies in our group said, "Hmmm. How bizarre." Curiously, everyone at the table was all ears. She then showed me a text she just received from her sister (whom I have never met) completely out of the blue. The text message, three verses from Psalms, is one I have been heavily leaning on the past two weeks.

"The Lord hears his people when they call to him for help. He rescues them from all their troubles. The Lord is close to the brokenhearted; he rescues those whose spirits are crushed. The righteous person faces many troubles, but the Lord comes to the rescue each time." Psalms 34: 17-19

Whether you are a believer or not, those are some incredibly powerful words, and to come at a time and in a way, clearly meant for me, was just downright goosebump-worthy.

Later in the evening, we ended up at a local café/late-night hot spot, Big Whiskey's. Two of Chuck's friends came up to the table where I sat, put their arms around me, and offered to buy a shot in honor of my recent loss, and their dear friend, Chuck. It was a tender moment with tears flowing freely and love for one who was no longer with us, bonding together those left behind.

I continue to look for answers to questions I will most likely never know.

Signs of his spirit surrounding me.

Comfort and peace from above and small shots of strength to face each new day without the love I came to know.

I vow to hold close to those precious messages and glimmers of hope that come when I least expect them.

They are my stepping stones, healing balm, and directional compass in this elusive journey toward peace.

RIP, Chuck Wiersch, March 2018

My Grandmother, the Dragonfly

by Amannda G. Maphies

Every time I see a dragonfly, I think of Grandma Joann Dolores Mann-Wadlow. She loved them. I have told the story (more than once) of the bittersweet day we auctioned the family farm.

Standing at the familiar wooden gate after the crowd dispersed, with tears in my eyes, recalling all the childhood and coming-of-age memories from the farm that now belonged to complete strangers, I happened to see a beautiful black and white dragonfly. Not an unordinary sighting in the July summer heat, I thought little of it, until the dragonfly literally landed on the gate, mere inches from my watery eyes.

She continued to flutter her iridescent wings, making a circle around the very ground in which I stood. It seemed to me, as if a messenger from Heaven, telling me everything would be fine. The house, all its contents and the surrounding 80 acres may no longer live in our family, but the treasured memories would last a lifetime.

My oldest son, Liam, who was probably around 7 at the time, silently walked up behind me. He stood still and looked at me for a long moment before asking why I was crying. I told him I was sad to say *Good-Bye* to my grandparents' farm. Trying to lighten the moment, I pointed to the dragonfly and said, "I think this is my grandma telling me all will be well and that she is at peace with this change."

Of course, my young, innocent son looked at me like I had grown a third head, a look I have come to know, then shrugged his little boy shoulders and followed the dragonfly with his little boy eyes, and very seriously said, "Well. There goes your grandma." I laughed. He laughed. I will never forget that moment in time.

I relish any opportunity I am fortunate to see a dragonfly, and often wonder what message she is delivering with each visit.

Chuck, My Guardian Golden Retriever

by Amannda G. Maphies

Several years ago, my aunt and I visited Chicago for a short get-away to indulge in some good old-fashioned rock and roll music, hosted by the *Rolling Stones* at the infamous Soldier Field. On our second evening in Chicago, as we were walking the very safe and friendly streets of downtown Chicago, we found the most beautiful Presbyterian Church. The stained-glass windows beckoned to me for photo opportunities and as I snapped pictures left and right, I noticed the church hosting an open-air market/craft festival right there on the sidewalk just outside the front doors. *Shocker:* I purchased my first piece of jewelry.

Still on a buyer's high (*I do not have a problem*), we continued our journey toward a welcoming Mexican cantina. As we neared the door to the restaurant, a man and his big beautiful golden retriever walked by.

My aunt, who does not know a stranger (especially when it comes to the four-legged, hairy, drooling, canine persuasion), made fast friends with the beautiful dog ... *and his owner*. I did not stop to pet him because I was more interested in the hole-in-the-wall cantina down the road as I knew they would be filling quickly and wanted to get an outdoor table. Thus, I kept walking. The dog, however, turned from his owner and proceeded to follow me as I walked in the opposite direction.

This friendly creature walked right up behind me and stood at my heels begging for a love. As I impatiently relented and turned to talk to him, offering a gentle pat, his owner loudly called, "*CHUCK!* Come here!"

Shaking my head in confusion and wondering if I had misheard the kind stranger, I asked if the dog's name was *Chuck*. The man kindly told me his name was *Charles*, but everyone calls him *Chuck*. My heart melted, as I thought back to the *Chuck* (Charles) I had known, loved, and lost less than a year prior to that trip.

Honestly, my travels with Chuck were some of the best times of my life. This incident served to remind me that while he may not be with me in person, he will always travel with me in spirit.

In memory of Charles (Chuck) Joseph Wiersch.
Gone, but never forgotten.

Message Out of the Blue

by Amannda G. Maphies

The messenger I long to see;
Sits stoically high upon his chosen tree.
I frantically pull over to the side;
In hopes a conversation he will abide.

He stares me down for a second or two;
Then flaps his long feathery tendrils.
He glides across the empty desolate field;
In search of shelter from the forest just beyond.

I am sure he perches on a lofty branch;
A post in which he sees my sad attempt.
Today is not the day he chooses to share;
The secrets of his fowl life and haunting, mysterious stare.

Every morning in this same mysterious spot;
I look for him, my messenger of the skies.
He evades my advances for a lengthy time;
But when I least expect, he will reveal himself to me once again.

This dance we have played for months, years to this day.
The same feathered being or a distant relative,
carrying out his fateful message to the world below.

Someday, my friend, we will meet again.
You with your lofty and secretive penetrating glare;
And me, with my curiosity aroused,
hoping to gain just a fraction of your otherworldly, mysterious
ways….

Chapter 6

Angelic Encounters

The Cry of the Loon

by Amannda G. Maphies

Why is your cry so mournful;
So high pitched and full of fear?
Are you missing your loved one;
The one you thought would always be here?

You fly around this very lake;
Day and night, I see you out.
But at night I hear that saddened cry;
It makes me want to scream and shout.

Something unfinished in your voice;
A message you didn't get to share.
An important thing for you to say;
But the recipient is no longer there.

So you mourn and you cry;
You restlessly circle the place.
This other half of you;
Took up so much time and space.

And now you are lonely;
Sad, blue, and depressed.
How will you go on;
Without the love you once professed?

The cry of the loon;
I know it so well.
I feel it so deeply;
I'm bound by its spell.

Common Loon

Legend

A Northern Water Bird that dives underwater easily . . . noted for its Wild Maniacal Laughing . . . Fossils date from 65 million years ago.

The Angel in Aisle Three

by Amannda G. Maphies

Years ago, I found myself in the local grocery store with my barely one year-old son. I wore an owl sweater covering my bony shoulders from weeks of eating as little as possible. My eyes were hollow with deep shadows of darkness underneath from countless nights of sleepless torture. My hair was crimped from braids the night before. It was the most I could do to exhibit an attempt at looking *ready* for public interaction and to face a new day.

My husband told me several weeks ago that he wanted a divorce. My kids were three and one year of age. I was heart-broken which quickly carried over to the anger and rage stage I stayed stuck in far too long. I was physically starved for food. Emotionally starved for love. And spiritually starved for understanding and peace from the constant pain in my chest from a world turned upside down in one single horrible conversation.

As I did my usual grocery shopping early that morning, I tried to put on my bravest face. If only for the small child smiling back at me from the front of the grocery cart. I needed to be strong for him, and his older brother. They were my saving grace during a time of traumatic emotional upheaval.

I recall walking to the dairy aisle, which I hated. It was cold, unwelcoming and made me want to shiver my way far from the butter, cheeses, and eggs seemingly mocking my awkward, troubled appearance. As I reached for a box of butter, I looked up to find an elderly gentleman directly beside me. *He looked kind.*

I smiled. He smiled. He looked me deep in my tired, sad, lifeless eyes said three simple words, *"You are beautiful."* Then he walked away. Tears streaming down my face, I turned to thank him. But he was gone. He vanished as quickly as he appeared. Changing my perspective, mood, and life, with three simple words.

At the depth of my despair, I entertained this angel unaware;
He touched my broken heart with words I will never forget.

He reached into my spirit and gave it a breath of re-birth;
Forcing me to rise above and re-evaluate my spiritual worth.

I will never know if he was really there, or a figment of my fractured imagination. I only know he brought a smile to my face and a song to my heart. *For the first time in weeks.*

I still had a long road to recovery and accepting my new normal. Yet, my interaction with the stranger on that particular day was the beginning of a healing path toward forgiveness, acceptance, peace, and a greater love than I had ever known. The experience changed the way I saw myself: as a rejected, empty, shell of a woman, to a beloved, worthy, precious, *beautiful* daughter of God.

I will always be thankful to the angel in Aisle Three.
I believe he was sent from Heaven above,
With a special message just for me.

*This story was previously published in Chicken Soup for the Soul:
Believing in Angels, January 2022

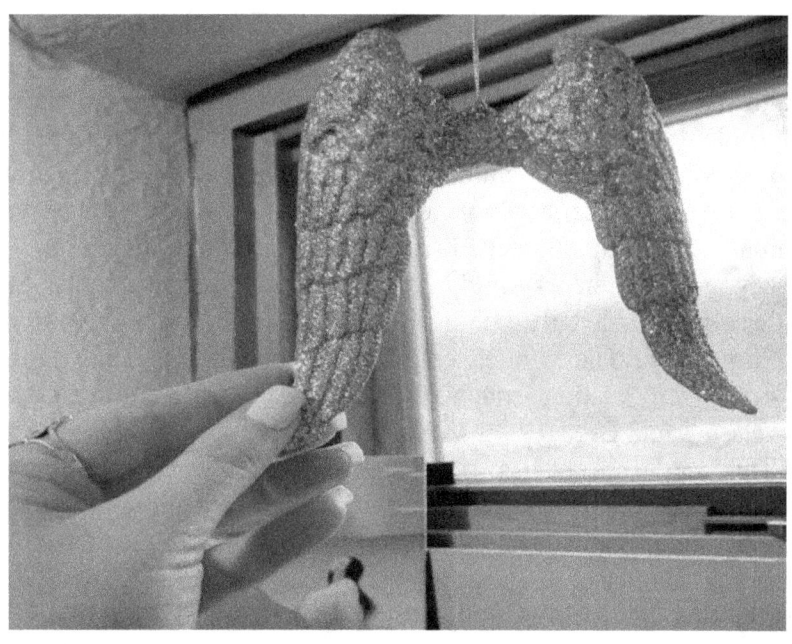

Angels in Santa Fe

by Amannda G. Maphies

One of my favorite places on earth is Santa Fe, New Mexico. Known by the locals as the *Land of Enchantment*, it is certainly that, and much, much more...

On our recent elopement trip in December 2021, our little home away from home turned out to be a tiny casita called *Casa de Angelos, House of the Angels*. I honestly cannot believe I didn't make this realization sooner, but my belief in angels has led me toward some definite inspired experiences over the years.

As I made a reservation for our little post-holiday get-away/elopement honeymoon package, I fell in love with this precious casa on Vacation Rental by Owner online. It looked tiny, but every nook and cranny was filled to the brim with reminders that angels abound in all areas of our human lives. Beloved pets that rescue us from the dredges of depression, strangers who magically appear at our designated hour of need, a friend we have not spoken to in years popping back into our lives at a majestically appointed time, a small child smiling deeply into our soul when we most need a moment of solace, a random encounter with a wild animal brings a much-needed feeling of comfort and protection.

My grandmother strongly inspired my belief in angels. She collected the heavenly beings in various figurines, photographs, paintings, etc. The winged celestial inhabitants filled her home, from floor to ceiling, much like the little Casa de Angeles we stayed in Santa Fe.

This one such angel at our casita in Santa Fe reminded me so much of my grandma. Her favorite salutation at the end of each card and letter was, *Love and Peace*. Little did I know, when I was snapping photos of the many angels occupying the space at our casita, this particular beauty, high upon a shelf, had the very destined word *"Peace"* engraved upon the bottom of her flowing gown. It was not until after I took the picture that I realized the message, which was precariously hidden at eye level.

Could it be my sweet grandmother, one of the most defining women in my life, is now an angel watching over me? I like to think so. She was certainly an angel on earth. How much more would she be an angel now, in her heavenly home, with her soulmate, my grandpa, in the much-anticipated arms of her Savior, *Jesus*.

Angels come in many forms. They may or may not be known to us at the time we encounter them. One of my favorite verses:

Do not forget to show hospitality to strangers, for by so doing some people have shown hospitality to angels without knowing it." Hebrews 13:2 (NIV)

This verse encapsulates the possibility that celestial beings may very well be walking the same path, and providing a fraction of the kindness, encouragement, and love our heavenly Father reveals in full, at our greatest time of need.

Angels abound in this life. The more we seek them, perhaps the greater chance we will be blessed to cross a divine heavenly-inspired angelic encounter.

Entertaining Angels Unaware

by Amannda G. Maphies

I recently went to get my nails done. As I was sitting in the chair, my faithful sensei (I may have binge-watched Cobra Kai this weekend) assured me the color I picked would be as dark as the sample (it looked way lighter in the jar). The lady sitting next to me looked over and said, "That's a good color for you. It matches your skin tone." I thanked her and absently turned my attention back to the Game Show Network.

When Raymond, my nail tech, put the last layer on my nails, my phone rang. It was my oldest son. I had to answer. Just as my nail tech screamed, *NOOOoooooo* (in slow-motion matrix style). I took the call. It wasn't urgent. But of course, I messed up one nail. *Royally.* Raymond shook his head and muttered something in another language. *I can only imagine ...*

The same lady who commented on my nail color asked, "How old is your son?" I answered, "I have two boys," and told her their ages. I further explained this was the first time I had left them alone and I was worried it was an emergency. (Turns out, they were just hungry. They are *always* hungry.) She laughed, after taking a call from her own son minutes after mine. She explained her son was twenty years old and after falling on some hard times due to Covid, had recently moved back home. She went on to tell me she had recently been diagnosed with her second bout of cancer. I told her I was so sorry. She cheerfully said, "Oh, don't be!" She went on to talk about her bond with her son and how protective he has always been of her, especially now, as she is fighting for her life.

I told her my boys are my world and I already fear them growing up, moving away, and forgetting about their crazy old mother. This stranger-turned-friend looked me square in the eye and said, "Honey. It won't happen. The bond between a mother and her son is unbreakable. They may physically move, but that bond will only strengthen in time." At this point, I was nearly in tears. How was a total stranger, in the nail salon I frequent at least twice a month, who is undergoing serious health issues, encouraging *me*?! Shouldn't it be the other way around...

I will not go so far as to say this woman was an angel. I also will not say she wasn't. What I will say, is she was the shot of strength, hope, and blessed assurance I needed on this day. I pray God gives her the continued strength to fight this battle. I also pray He blesses her for blessing others, as today she touched my heart in a way only one of God's precious children could.

I have said it before, you never know the impact you could have on someone, just by being kind.

"1 Keep on loving one another as brothers and sisters. 2 Do not forget to show hospitality to strangers, for by so doing some people have shown hospitality to angels without knowing it." Hebrews 13:1-2 (NIV)

Unexpected Angels

by Amannda G. Maphies

Sometimes life's unexpected toils turn out to be life's sweetest treats.

I took my car in for an oil change today. Five hours later, they are still diagnostically testing various things, including two shotty tires (that I am not financially prepared to replace this month). Fortunately, I had the foresight to catch a shuttle from the dealership to my office before I knew this would be an all-afternoon affair.

The shuttle driver was the nicest gentleman. After telling him my whole life story (he seemed a little stunned ... perhaps fearful), he revealed to me that he is a published author. *What are the chances?*

I told him I am an aspiring author but have not made it past the creative planning/plotting/writing stage. He practically threw his book (I insisted on an autographed copy) into my lap and proceeded to give me pointers on next steps for publishing. *For real?!*

What a perfectly amazing divine intervention with a complete stranger/possible angel/friendly alien on earthly sabbatical. As if I was not already on cloud nine, I arrived at the dealership to find that the two tires in dire need of replacement will be covered under warranty by the exceptional folks at Youngblood Nissan. Where they surely treat you like family! (Wait, no....that's the *Olive Garden*). Same sentiment applies though!

What started off as a crappy day has turned into mounting blessings that has my spirit as giddy as a young boy with a nerf gun and a sleeping brother! From pesky pitfall to bountiful delight, I love that life's tough moments can change on a dime to reveal treasured gifts in the most unexpected places.

Chapter 7

Tales from Another Room

Mystical Nights

by Amannda G. Maphies

There is a certain strangeness hanging heavy in the air;
A dark and penetrating force beyond compare.
Hiding itself from the light of day;
Yet revealing its incessant energy to those heightened with ultra-
sensitivity to that region just outside the known.

The fullness of the moon;
Blood orange and ominous shining over the horizon.
The stillness of the night;
Pierced by a raven's morose sting, which cuts the silent air.

This discreet message begs to be revealed;
Yet shrouds itself in mystery, hiding like a panther of the night,
awaiting the perfect moment to strike its innocent prey.
The intensity catches me in a vice;
Stunned paralyzed by the need to know, coupled with the inability
to grasp the answers just outside my forceful grip.

The sundry Seminole wields her righteous claim;
Rendering me helpless, confused, and hungering for knowledge of
what is soon to come.
The mocking laugh of the jackal in the distance;
Revealing my discontent, my plight at knowing life is strained, but
without the heavy knowledge in which I need to cope.

Just one hint, one clue of future catastrophe;
Is all I humbly beg of thee.
Or, is it best to plunder on in darkness;
Praying for intervention to release this heavy need?

The Honeymoon

by William Amherst DeBoef, age 11

Once upon a time, there was a man. This man was living alone at the time, when he met the love of his life and moved in with her.

They went on their honeymoon after they got married. They did not know, however, that it would be their last trip together.

They flew to a place in California. For the first few days, everything was normal. But then they went to the beach…and this is where things started to get weird.

They heard a piano playing from their beachside resort. The woman insisted the man stay, but he went to check out the resort, where he met a man who was willing to give the newly married man $10,000 if he signed a paper.

He signed the paper. The man snickered and said, "Have a great day." The man then walked back to his partner. The man who was at the resort, we will call him Jim, in his human form. However, this man was a demon who had made the man on the honeymoon sign his soul to the devil.

When the man and his wife went to bed, Jim, in his demon form, dragged the man and his wife away, where they were thought to be tortured. People say that this demon still goes to resorts to find his next victim.

The Aproned Lady

by Carrie Kendall

She sits in the same spot for lunch every day. Pristine and always in low heels, she smiles courteously at the attendant waiting at the end of the buffet line. After she puts her card in her apron pocket, she tucks the curl of an ashy blonde lock behind her left ear. I watch her like a mother checks on a sleeping baby; curiously, but certain to never let her know I am there.

Her mannerisms are always the same. Put the tray down. Place a napkin in her lap, and one in her left hand. A big sigh, and then the first bite. She eats a variety of foods for lunch, but always chooses a small dish of vanilla soft serve for dessert. Oddly, she only ever takes one spoonful, and then lifts the grey tray stamped *Lighthouse Independent Living* off the table and carries it to the cafeteria's moving belt. After depositing her tray, she swipes the curl again and walks to the sunroom, just to the east of the cafe.

I have lived here fourteen years. My soulmate died six months ago. One night I told her I was staying up late, and the next morning, there she lie, motionless in our bed. I was shocked to see her there, as she has always risen before me to tend to something unknown before the sun came up. That morning, she looked as silent as Snow White waiting for her Prince to kiss her. So that is what I did. I leaned over and kissed her forehead. I knew right away she was gone. Our life together had come to an end.

Now, I spend most of my time in the sunroom. I usually trot in to watch the sunrise at 5:30 a.m. with Mr. Taylor. There are lounge chairs nobody uses because they are too hard to get out of, three white wooden rocking chairs, and two electric recliners. The remaining seating is generic plastic folding chairs. All of the chairs face the wall of floor-to-ceiling windows, where the sunrise is displayed for an hour and then the massive blinds are drawn by the push of a button, so as not to blind the viewers when the sun is at eye level.

Sitting there, I am often overcome by Mr. Taylor's fresh scent of *Old Spice* aftershave. Still, I sit next to him, and he talks about the weather as if we haven't known each other for more than a decade. Just the two of us, we each get our own seat, the best in the house. When he goes to get coffee, I wait for Joe Pipkin. He always shuffles in with his coffee in a cupholder on his walker and a newspaper tucked under his arm. He always chooses the newly vacant recliner next to me. He gets right into the paper, so we don't say much.

Natalie Cransford comes in at 6:15 a.m. like clockwork. She pats us on the back, *"Good morning, Max, Joe,"* then starts getting the room ready for the morning exercises. Most of us old guys know that is our cue to move on, but every now and then I stick around. All the exercise is done from the chair, anyway.

I have never seen the aproned lady in morning exercise class. She doesn't need to, though. She has a perfect figure, like the original Barbie Doll. Time has been kind to her appearance. You can't see the wrinkles most people her age have by now. In fact, she looks and moves around more like a 50-year-old, if you ask me, but I know she is at least 55, because you have to be, to live here. In fact, most of the residents are in their 70s and 80s. I suppose that is why I have noticed her now. She is a standout in this crowd.

This morning, after exercise class finished, I heard the piano in the lobby. Only three people ever play it: Norman, the director of activities, Joe's wife, Judith, and Patty Mayfield.

Patty is phenomenal, and it sounds like her fingers are doing the walking today, so I make my way to the open-air lobby. The blinds have not been drawn yet, as the sun is in this room in the late afternoon, so the natural light is perfect for the pianist. There are four polka-dot patterned armchairs and a coffee table arranged in a diamond in front of the piano. I choose the chair closest to the piano and close my eyes.

Today's player has chosen a selection of songs from *The Sound of Music*. I have always loved that music and began to daydream about my younger years, running next to a faithful bike rider on the streets after primary school. After Edelweiss, the playing stopped and I heard someone sneeze, which startled me from my daydreaming.

When I opened my eyes, I saw the aproned lady, standing right in front of me. Shocked, I motioned to get up, but she patted my head and said, *"It's okay, Max. We can share the seat."* So, I rolled to my back, and offered my belly for rubs. Sometimes I wonder if other dogs get as much love as me.

The Things We Leave Behind

by Amannda G. Maphies

This past weekend I took my little black cockapoo, Atlas, for a short outdoor walk to the creek behind our home in Joplin, Missouri. While it was far too cold to be concerned about ticks and snakes, there was a healthy population of *sticky grass* assaulting the legs of my little canine sidekick and myself. It was an Indian summer's day in the midst of winter. The blue sky overhead had barely a cloud in sight. The wind was a formidable force, but the feel of the bright warm sunshine on my bare face was a welcome winter delight.

As we neared the flowing water's edge, I noticed a group of turkeys on the other side of the river. Unfortunately, Atlas noticed them around the same time I did. One bark was all it took. The turkeys took off in a panic and flew from one side of the river to the other, awkwardly landing and continuing to run quickly into the woods beyond my vision.

As I stood, watching the last turkey take cover in the woods beyond the river, my dog was already in hot pursuit of another scent unbeknownst to me. As I followed him, we came upon a bright orange hunting cap, lying lifeless in the tall grass just feet from the water's murky edge.

Curious as to how someone loses their stocking cap, I assumed there was a dramatic story behind the lost hat, and awkwardly stepped into the unmanicured tall grass in search of the body I was certain was lying nearby.

My dog bounded in and out of the grass, enjoying the many scents the trail offered. I kept my eyes peeled for the dead body I was apprehensive, but slightly excited, to find. It was nowhere in sight. Until, something shining in the glistening sun, out of the corner of my eye, caught my already heighted attention. It was a hand. A small, white hand, with a silver ring on the pointer finger. It was awkwardly poking out of the large bushes in the near distance. I slowly walked toward the hand, apprehensive of what might (or might not) be attached.

As I arrived at the exposed hand, I pulled back a large tuft of grass to reveal what I feared the most. A body. A female body. It was caked in mud, with traces of dried water and grass revealing only bits and pieces of what would become my worst nightmare. As I wiped the dirt away, I was startled to find the dirty, murky, muddy, lifeless face staring back at me was...*my own.*

As the immediate shock transitioned to an abhorrent reaction, I started to scream. My screams quickly turned to sobs. The tears pooling in my eyes trickled down my cheeks to land on the face staring back at me, revealing my very own deeply set and now lifeless blue eyes.

With each steady tear that fell, a trace of this life was revealed. Her body was tattooed with a map of her life. Some roads revealing deep hurt and suffering, others showcasing a season of joy, excitement, and passion.

In that moment, I understood the pattern revealed to me, slowly and with each tear trickling down my face onto the lifeless body before me, was not just a pattern. It was my life. The ghost of my former self awaiting the fated kiss of release from the present me kneeling over the body signifying that which was no more.

As I released a flood of emotion, I heard a ruffle of feathers behind my kneeling form. I turned to see an owl land. He stared intently into my eyes. His own eyes, deep cavities of infinite wisdom, challenging me to seek the truth revealed in the former part of me long passed away. I realized that which we know fills only a fraction of the vacuum compared to that which will one day be revealed to our higher sense of self.

It occurred to me, the owl was not there to provide answers. He was simply there to reveal the infinite space of understanding in which I had yet to arrive. He carried with him a deep spiritual message I cannot adequately describe in words, but the feeling is one I will never forget. An understanding. An awakening. A release of electricity sent shivers from my own present human beating heart to the lifeless form lying on the ground inches from my muddy feet.

There was a journey. One with no particular end, but a very

definitive beginning. A journey of growth, healing, passions revealed, past sins forgiven and future hope gaining momentum with each passing breath.

I saw the lifeless face in front of me suck in a large deep breath. The blue hue around her skin turned to sparkly crystal white. The tracks of pain dissipated, and in their wake, a shimmery, transparent effervescence of beauty remained. This lifeless soul. This *me*...was given freedom from imprisonment by every solitary tear I shed, which landed squarely upon her face.

I covered my face in my hands and I mourned for this soul. This past version of me, with her hurt and her pain and her great awakening and vision of hopes and dreams for her future. When I removed my hands from my tear-stained face, the body in front of me had disappeared into the ether. There was a faint glow of effervescence left in her wake, plunging me back to reality and wondering if what I had just witnessed was only a figment of my overactive imagination.

I turned to seek answers from the owl. But he, too, had vanished into thin air. No sound to alert me of his passage through time. Only one feather remained, along with the bright orange hunter's cap which heightened my senses to the onset of this whole mystifying adventure only minutes before.

As I gathered a bout of strength to rise up from the grass holding me hostage to the cold, hard ground, I turned to walk back toward the house. I emerged from the trees, with their wooded secrets the river revealed to me that day.

I walked slowly past the remaining bright orange hunter's cap, feet from where I emerged. A stark reminder that what is left behind only remains until we face the heartache, claim forgiveness, and forge ahead toward our fateful destiny.

The orange cap was the only thing that remained ...

Chapter 8

Childhood Memories

The Empty Swing

by Amannda G. Maphies

Swinging on the wind;
Back and forth, to and fro.
The empty swing holds a secret;
Only few on earth will ever know.

Years ago, the swing was made;
By the daddy of a little girl.
It brought such joy and excitement on those summer days;
When she would fly through the air, with not a care in the world.

That little girl grew up;
She sought to move away.
She had a family of her own;
Little children longing to daily play.

She took those little children;
To the familiar home in which she once lived.
That swing was still hanging on the old walnut tree;
Still flowing freely on the wind.

She hopped up on the swing;
Let her momma defenses down.
She showed her children a different sight;
The little girl they never knew.

She sang her favorite songs;
She daydreamed with visions of allure.
She pondered the purpose of this life;
She recalled the years of her misspent youth.

Something harsh entered her perimeter;
A dark and menacing threat.
Her eyes flew open to look around;
She was no longer living in that safe memory.

Now she sat in darkness;
Haunted by the former joy she knew.
That swing still fresh upon her mind;
Enchantment danced in her reminiscent days.

Oh! How she longed to swing again;
Not a care left in this world.
She yearned for simpler days to come;
Transporting her to that once familiar little girl.

Dorrie, the Witch

by Amannda G. Maphies

Long before Harry Potter or the Twilight series, there was a simple little girl named Dorrie. Dorrie was a witch. And I loved her.

Last night, despite a messy house and my normal daily tasks not being complete, I decided to throw caution to the wind and decorate anyway. Halloween is one of my absolute favorite times of year. The mystery, the adorable children's costumes, the mouth-watering and tooth-decaying candy, the pumpkins, the scary movies, I truly love it all.

As I was pulling my décor out of the garage, it occurred to me that I have collected several of these books over the years, *Dorrie the Witch*. This was my favorite series as a child. I remember going to my hometown library on endless summer days with my mother. Always anticipating a new Dorrie book I had not read. The best was when my mom would sit down and read them with me. (I think she may have enjoyed them as much as I did).

I always related to Dorrie, the Little Witch. She was awkward and messy. She tried desperately to manage the spells her mother was adept at, yet she continually messed up and produced more havoc and chaos than humanly possible. Or, I should say *witchingly* possible. Thus, her mother would fly to the rescue and clean up Dorrie's mess. Her mother was constantly exasperated with her only daughter. Yet, there was an air of pride and patient anticipation that Dorrie would one day, master her witchy craft.

Never far away from her trusty black cat, Gink. Dorrie's adventures transferred me miles away from my sleepy hometown summers into a world of magic, mayhem, comedy, and at times, very dark and mysterious lands. It is no wonder Halloween is one of my favorite holidays. These books hold a piece of my childhood and represent the wild imagination and vivid artistry coloring many of my first years.

Upon digging them out early this morning, to add to my already overflowing Halloween collection, I vowed to read each and every one with my sons. Oh sure, they will squirm with discomfort. I can hear them now. "Mom! It's about a GIRL witch…*NO!!!!*" I do think the black cat will be a selling factor for my youngest as he is obsessed with our very own resident black cat, Hamilton. And I can always bribe the older child with candy or soda…

Good Intentions

by Amannda G. Maphies

This morning I was contemplating good intentions. Prompted by a story I recently shared with a friend, I made a connection and wanted to write about it.

When I was around six years old, my dad took me quail hunting. He had his trusty Brittany Spaniel, *Suzi*, along with our brand-new English Setter pup, *Sami*, in tow. He also had two live baby quail in a small tin pail, as he was working with young Sami on her emerging hunting skills.

Little Manndi, a young bleeding heart, if ever there was one, felt compelled to *free* the baby birds. Waiting for just the right moment, she opened the lid to the container and out flew baby bird #1, followed closely by baby bird #2. What happened next was completely unexpected and equally tragic to the heroic freedom-fighter of my youth.

Suzi, a svelte-looking Brittany, jumped high in the air, grabbing baby bird #1 and hungrily crunching down like a dog with a bone. Or rather, *a dog with a baby bird*. Sami, young and spry, also leaped toward the babies, grabbing the one left after Suzi made her selection. This happened in a period of seconds.

With bones crunching and blood dripping down the chops of my two furry companions, I was stunned, abhorred, traumatized and...afraid to look at my Daddy! Of course, I heard what would become the infamous, *"MANN-DI!"*, only Duane Maphies can orate with true precision.

I sheepishly turned to look at my father, tears in my eyes and fear in my heart. I could tell his frustration was real, yet his grace was sufficient. He knew my childish mistake had resulted in breaking my own heart. And like our heavenly Father, he allowed me to learn a lesson about patience, trust, and obedience that I will never forget. My dad was slow to anger and quick to forgive.

I learned a very valuable lesson that day. The best of intentions do not always produce the desired results. Especially, if we step out on our own and avoid wise direction.

Yet.

Grace and forgiveness is always available when we seek it and vow to learn from our mistakes. I am so incredibly thankful for an earthly father who taught me so much about my heavenly Father. While I was not exactly invited to hunt again (at least not with training birds), the lesson I learned that day, and the love I felt when I knew I had messed up royally, is a gift I will carry in my heart until my last day.

Overhearing an Important Conversation

by Amannda G. Maphies

When I was a little girl, my parents attended Countryside Christian Church in Monett, Missouri. It was a small country church set upon a big hill on the outskirts of our small town. We liked to think of our small yet growing congregation as the "light upon a hill," sharing the news of Jesus with our small-town, close-knit community.

Since the church was small and only operated based on tithes from the members and an occasional gracious donation, our church had no funds for a custodial crew. Thus, each member was assigned a month to clean the church in its entirety, which included a sanctuary, with a full basement underneath, where all the children's Sunday School classes were housed.

As a child, I would go with my mom to *help* her clean. I wasn't really much help, but I was at the age where staying out of the way was more helpful to her than *actually* helping. So, I would explore the empty church, which seemed a bit creepy since I was used to only being there on Sunday mornings when there was a full sanctuary of people.

I would also practice my piano lessons at the front of the sanctuary on the light-grained wooden piano we used for the song service on Sunday mornings. On one such occasion, I was sitting at the piano bench, playing my recently assigned piano lesson, when I heard a muffled sound beyond the door just feet away from where I sat at the piano. Behind the stage was the minister's office, the entrance to the baptistry, and an enclosed balcony which had plans for an expansion in the future. I was not supposed to go in that area since the preacher may or may not have been there working on his weekly sermon notes.

Curious what the muffled voice was, I stopped tickling the ivories and pressed my ear up to the wooden door. I could have sworn I heard the voice of a man in our congregation. This man was a young single adult member of our church. He was the son of a lovely couple who attended the church on occasion. Their son, however, was there every time the church doors were open. He was a bit of an odd character, but with a heart of gold and everyone who knew him, loved him.

When I stopped playing the piano and listened intently, I was sure it was the distinct voice of this man I heard. I thought it rather odd he would be in that room, which was the preacher's office, all by myself (I am not sure to this day if the preacher was there or not).

For some reason, this experience really unnerved my little girl heart and mind. As an only child, who had an overactive imagination, I shared nearly everything (good, bad, ugly, made-up and true) with my parents. *Except for this.* Something told me this was a secret I was not meant to overhear, and I must keep it to myself. *So, I did.*

For years, I had this image of this sweet man, locked in the front of the church, overlooking the parking lot below, on his knees, pouring his heart out to the God he searched every Sunday morning to find. He seemed distressed in my vision. I always felt uneasy when I recalled this memory.

This young man, obviously fighting bigger demons than his family and friends knew at the time, committed suicide not long after I heard his voice. As an adult, this event has plagued me from time to time, wondering if I could have helped by telling someone what I heard. For all I know, he could have been speaking with the minister about the struggles on his heart. He could have been talking to God about how he simply could not cope in this world any longer. Perhaps, he was not even there on that fateful day, and the voice I heard was some sort of divine connection with the tragedy soon to come. I really have no idea.

The only resolution I have found from this experience is that I heard the distinct voice of a man I know loved Jesus. I am hopeful he was praying to a God he knew he would soon meet face-to-face. I cannot say what went through his mind when he did the unthinkable. I can only believe, in my heart of hearts, he did everything in his power to prepare his heart to meet his Lord.

A Tribute to Nancy Drew

by Amannda G. Maphies

I grew up reading Nancy Drew mysteries. One of many traits I inherited from my mother is my love for a good mystery coupled with some light romance on the side. Written at a time when women took a more behind-the-scenes role to men, Nancy Drew would have nothing of the sort. She had a gift for sniffing out mysteries, and a penchant for successfully solving them, with or without the help of her lawyer father and boyfriend-in-training, Ned. *Oh Ned...what a silly boy he was!*

At one of my favorite times of year, with Halloween breathing patiently to unleash the trick-or-treaters, with my senses for all things eerily spooky properly heightened, I often overlook the blood-covered zombies and heavily made-up B-grade horror flick characters. My eyes tend to hone-in on abandoned houses, old-school 50s and 60s inspired costumes, timeless black and white movies such as *The Ghost and Mrs. Muir* and the original *House on Haunted Hill*, starring the legendary Vincent Price.

Like Nancy, my deeply intrinsic desire is to solve the world's mysteries, or perhaps contribute to the mystery of the world. Most creepy experiences can be explained by rational terms. It is the few which cannot, that pique my inner sleuth and mysterious thirst for *that which cannot be explained*, that most intrigue my otherworldly senses.

Happy Halloween to all of you ghostly ghouls out there. May the mystery of this day, and night, fill you with a childish wonder and a captivating curiosity toward all that is *BOO-ti-ful*.

Chapter 9

Dreams, Visions, and Whispers

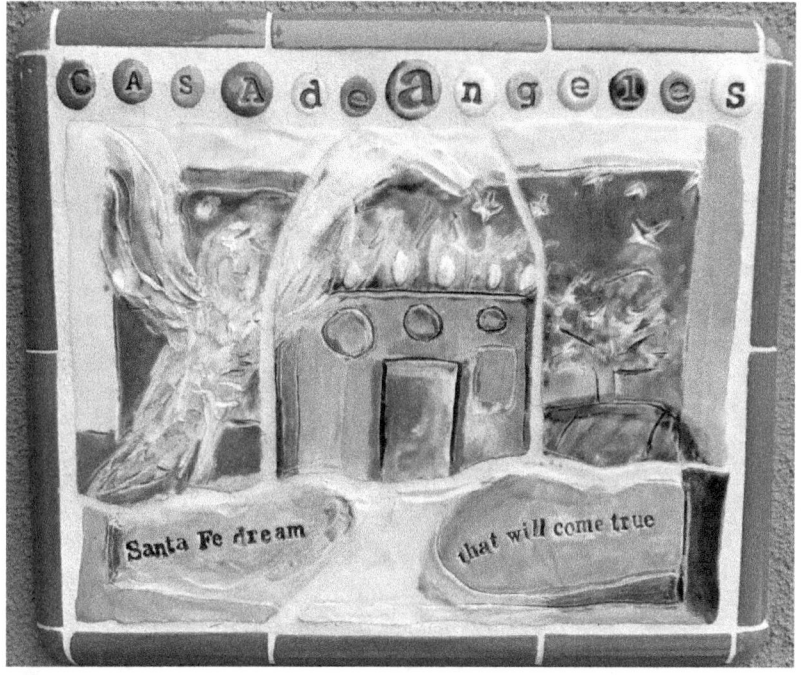

Feathers

by Amannda G. Maphies

Finding feathers on my path,
A sign of angels in my grasp.
Protection comes in many ways;
The love once shared will never fade.

Never would I think of you,
Distant, quiet, cold, and blue.
A force with which to reckon with,
You never would have jumped this ship.

I know it was not in your plan,
To go and leave me here alone.
I miss you deeply, everyday;
Your voice, your jokes, your gentle way.

We move, we force ourselves to breathe;
To gratify the urgent need.
Life goes on in simple ways,
The need for you will never change.

Finding feathers on my path,
A sign that love will always last.
A reminder you are not really gone,
A cloak of love from the great beyond.

Dream, Vision or Nightmare?

by Amannda G. Maphies

I had the most terrifying and simultaneously realistic dream of my life last night. As horrible as it was, I wanted to record it before the memory started to fade and the fear dissipates into the inaccessible dark recesses of the dream-catching portion of my brain.

It was a beautiful autumn day. I was hanging out with my boyfriend at a local park (it faintly resembled a historic farm not far from my house). Yet there were acres of uninhabited land. We were amongst many others, enjoying the perfect fall weather out of doors. A hint of chill in the air to signify winter coming, yet comfortable enough in the moment not to care. We were doing pirouettes in the grass, a very *Sound of Music-esque* scene. (Not something I typically do on an autumn afternoon (or *any* afternoon), but it seemed quite normal in my dream.)

The calm, tranquil, laid-back perfection of the day started to shift with an ominous forewarning of evil lurking just around the bend. I spotted what appeared to be a fighter jet in the distance, roaring with pride as it grew closer in proximity to the area of public green space we were enjoying. I pointed the jet out to my boyfriend. We reveled at the size of the machine, the sound it elicited, and the sheer power and force bursting from the engine.

Our collective awe quickly turned to confusion, followed by panic, as one single fighter jet multiplied before our very eyes. The horizon within our view morphed from one to many fighter jets in a single solitary line, perfectly arranged side-by-side and heading straight for the area in which we were standing.

In an instant, one of the jets dropped a single bomb. The flight through the air was stalled in slow motion, eliciting panic and terror in every onlooker present. The one bomb turned to five, then ten. Before I registered the frightening reality of the situation, the whole sky was filled with smoke. A horrid burning smell filled the air and the panic of those on foot was as heavy and stifling as a weighted blanket on the hottest of summer days. People began to scatter in every direction. Yelling at loved ones to run, hide, stay together, or spread apart. It was mass chaos. I was rendered helpless and paralyzed by confusion and fear.

My boyfriend grabbed my hand and we both started to run. I tried desperately to keep up, not knowing where we were headed, but thankful to have someone take charge. I did not allow myself to glance at the sky, for fear of what I would see there. I kept a straight-line tunnel vision on my boyfriend and the path directly ahead of us.

After running for what seemed like hours, we came to an empty field. My legs felt like jelly, my lungs burned from a combination of smoke and the bitter chill in the air. Still seeing and hearing the mutiny in the background, the field somehow seemed eerily quiet. Like a safe haven amongst the war in the distance.

We slowed our pace to catch our breath and within the distant line of sight, a familiar looking house slowly and steadily morphed into view. It was a house I knew, but I was not sure why. It seemed familiar, yet simultaneously haunted, deserted, and foreboding. A safe harbor of hope, filled with ghosts from my past. I was thankful for the source of relief, yet filled with anxiety as to what may be lurking inside.

The closer we came to the old structure, the more familiar it seemed. Finally, it dawned upon me why I knew this house. It was my grandparent's farm, a house I knew quite well from my youth, but had long since been sold from our family's history. The house bore a faint resemblance to the home I knew as a child, yet held a dark and foreboding air, which somehow haunted me more than the bomb smoke smoldering at my back.

We entered the house. My boyfriend secured the doors and windows while I curiously looked around for signs of life in the seemingly abandoned farmhouse once full of life, laughter, and cheer.

There was a basement which may provide protection. My boyfriend assured me if a bomb was to strike anywhere near our location, it did not matter if we were in the basement or on the roof, we would be dead in seconds. I found that somewhat a consolation…*NOT!*

I drug my tired and heavy body down the stairs to the dark basement lying in wait. I felt an overwhelming urge to contact my parents. After dialing the familiar number, my dad answered immediately. I told him I loved him; that I did not know what was happening but that if we didn't make it, I would see him on the other side. I then asked to speak with my mom. The phone went dead. I was heartbreakingly denied the same semblance of closure with one of the two most important people in my life.

Forming a semi-logical pattern in my mind, I startled upon the realization that my sons were still in school. *I needed to get to them!* No matter how safe, secure, and isolated our location, I needed to venture back into the bomb smoke, deafening sounds of aircraft, distant screams, and cries for help. I needed to get to my children, no matter the cost to my own life. *They* became my will to survive.

I ran up the stairs with newfound vigor, explaining to my boyfriend that we had to find a vehicle and get to the boys' school. He ran out of the house; I could only assume in an effort to find said vehicle so we could be on our way. I walked outside to the familiar front porch I knew as a child. What once symbolized a meeting place of tranquility, pleasure, laughter, community, and love, was now surrounded by barbs of evil, smoke rising in the distance, sounds of torture and human hatred filling the air. The mayhem was getting closer by the minute. It felt like it would soon be upon us.

What seemed like hours later, I saw a vehicle traveling down the gravel lane at Mach speed. It was my boyfriend, driving a gray Dodge Ram (ironically, he *does* drive a gray Dodge Ram in the non-dream world). He barely stopped for me to hop inside. He thrust his foot on the gas and violently threw gravel every direction behind the truck. We sped into town, bombs dropping in the rearview mirror like a horror movie, smoke filling the highway and making it difficult to see ahead. Cries of pain and suffering filling every vacant atom of sound in the distance. It was a nightmare unrivaled by any I have ever known.

The strong desire to control the situation, yet the helpless knowledge painfully reminding me I could not. Any minute one of those distant bombs could strike me, my family, and everyone I have ever known or loved, into unknown oblivion.

That is where the dream ended. No closure found in being reunited with my children. I was on my way to them, but did not make it before I woke and sleepily tried to separate reality from the nightmare I had just endured. Why is it that the most unsettling, horrifying dreams are the ones we cannot help but dissect in efforts to arrive at a plausible meaning?

Was it just my subconscious trying to make sense of some random statements I have heard or read lately on social media and in the news due to the world-wide pandemic? Was it a deep-seeded, underlying fear of civil unrest in our country and where it could lead? Or, was it just a random, illogical series of images in my mind holding no rhyme or reason whatsoever?

I believe dreams usually do hold some form of meaning, a morsel of truth. Whether they come as a warning or serve as a wake-up call to pursue a previously procrastinated life task. I believe they hold messages from deep within the untapped part of our brain which normally only functions when awake.

I typically do not recall the details of my dreams. On occasion, I will awake recalling what visions played out in my subconscious. This dream, however, is still as vividly real days later, as it was the morning I woke up and replayed the unsettling series of events. I genuinely hope this dream was simply a manifestation of the political unrest days after the presidential election, and not a foreshadowing of evil, violence, and terroristic attacks yet to come.

Sorrow, Sewing and Seven Stairs

by Dr. Melinda Hammerschmidt

When I was first married, I had a wonderful older lady in the community who would sew for me. She became a cherished friend, Mrs. Smith. Mrs. Smith was a very talented seamstress who could simply look at a picture and produce a brilliant work of art. My home was filled with lovely things Mrs. Smith made for us: a bedspread, table runners, and a Christmas tree skirt which I still use to this day.

Mrs. Smith also sewed for my son and put together the darling outfits I hand-smocked. She got great joy out of seeing Robert, my first son, wear his little outfits. Mrs. Smith was a very caring and loving wife to her husband. When he passed away, she expressed an interest in travel with some of her local friends from church. She anxiously awaited the bus trip they had planned to view the fall foliage in all of its splendor. Mrs. Smith took the trip, enjoyed a wonderful adventure, and talked of going on more trips. Sadly, it turned out this would be the last earthly trip she would make.

After returning from her vacation, we scheduled a time to meet the following day, Thursday, to visit about the trip and put the finishing touches on a fall outfit for Robert. On Wednesday, in the late afternoon, she was driving her little car to pick up her friends for church, when a sudden torrential downpour started. Visibility was very low as she turned on to the highway and was hit by an oncoming car.

The three ladies passed away instantly.

I was distraught that I had lost my friend and remember being inconsolable as we went to bed that evening. During the night, I had a vivid dream of my sweet friend and mentor.

Mrs. Smith was sitting on the landing of a beautiful white marble-looking staircase. There were seven stairs leading up to the landing where she was sitting, with seven more stairs ascending behind her, and the stairway appeared to continue endlessly.

Mrs. Smith had a large basket sitting on her lap. She was holding fabric, along with a threaded needle. As I approached her to say hello, she smiled and very clearly said, "Melinda, it's going to be alright."

I awoke and felt a huge burden had been lifted from my heart.

Chapter 10

Autumn Magic

The Beauty of Autumn

by Amannda G. Maphies

To the bright and colorful leaf;
Floating on the breezy wind.
Who does not know from where she started;
With no reason at all to fear the end.

I sense your freedom in the breeze;
I feel your soft landing upon the path.
Once attached to a strong and rugged branch;
Now you cleave to find your freedom, letting go and falling fast.

Your story is one unique only to you;
Once nothing but a bud residing on a naked stick.
Then growth translated to a full and healthy leaf;
Adorning the branch you claimed as your own.

The transition of a season colored you with time;
A beauty of vibrance not to be compared.
But standing tall and proud on her own;
A beauty beyond all others' unaware.

Then autumn fills the changing air;
Your friends have started to emerge.
Letting go of the safety always known,
Gracefully paving the forest floor;
Providing refuge and warmth to the residents of this wood.

To start from nothing and traverse all phases;
My soul feels tied to this cycle of life.
To grow, to change, to be and bear;
A song so timeless of blessing so rare.

The magic of autumn and one solitary leaf riding the gentle breeze from treetop to trail prompted me to write this poem.

Transition

by Amannda G. Maphies

I love the trees that show the progression of autumn. From green supple healthy growth to fiery shades of orange to blinding shades of red. The leaves are most vibrant and breathtaking just before taking their final plummet to the ground, where they become crispy, crunchy, dried-up versions of what once held such captivating color.

Very much in tune to the human spirit. Starting out fresh, green, full of wonder and little knowledge on which to stand. Growing to a vibrant full-spirited teenager with excitement and energy in vast reserve. Further morphing into a middle-aged leaf, showing her splendor for all the world to see. Brighter than a burning bush with passion coming in full force, and an acceptance of self only accrued after years of awkward stumbling in the dark.

Finally, she lets loose. She floats daintily to the ground. Carried on the chill of autumn breeze which warns of winter's icy fingers soon to come. She lies, lifeless, on the ground. A life full and vibrant waiting for her final breath. Her life is now complete. Her home void and empty of the bounty it once so artfully displayed.

She lets go. She rests. She fades into the earth and her once beautiful glow morphs into a rich story of nurturing wisdom, filling the cold, hard, brittle ground with a hint of new life inevitably waiting for the cycle to once again...*begin.*

Moon Child

by Amannda G. Maphies

I have never been called a *moon child*, per say, yet I relate to the moon far more than the sun. The sun shines brightly every single day. Even when shrouded by rain clouds or winter weather systems moving in, the sun is shining brightly wherever she is able, whether visible to our limited human eyes or not. The moon, however, only shows herself in phases. The phases of the moon have always fascinated me.

Just this morning, I saw the tiniest crescent of light, appearing like a fingernail clipping, dotting the slowly awakening sky. I took a picture, but you can scarcely see the target of new moon developing in her monthly phase of waxing and waning. I relate to the moon. At times, I am quite full and luminescent, casting a far-reaching glow in my small corner of the world. At other times, I feel less than the picture I saw this morning, a mere slice of faint light barely making her presence known in a world moving too swiftly for me to take hold and be present. A hidden vessel of barely visible light, hiding behind the overshadowing clouds in the dark of night.

"But the path of the righteous is like the light of dawn, which shines brighter and brighter until full day." Proverbs 4:18 (ESV)

I realize this verse is in reference to the rising sun and full shining force that peaks at noon each day. But I think it can apply to the moon as well. In the life of a Christian, we start out as a small, miniscule, crescent of light, growing brighter and fuller with each passing season of life. Until one day, we reach the apex, successfully shining brighter than ever before, and perhaps only for a brief time, until we again start to wane toward the lower lighted crescent we once were.

Weariness, life's inevitable battles, personal or familial health issues, parenting and relationship woes, all common factors dulling our shine, causing us to appear less than full.

Yet.

If we stay in step with the Lord, seek him daily, ask Him for peace from the rumble of the world and rest from the weariness felt in our souls, He *will* provide. He will take us by the hand and walk us toward a new season of growth, maturity, and yes, fully cascading and beautifully illuminating light.

How is your moon shining at present? Are you a half moon, waxing moon, waning moon, full moon? Whatever phase of life you are in, know that with the pull of the tides your heavenly Father so magically constructed in all things earth, nature, galaxy and humanity, your phase *will* no doubt change. It may grow *less*; it may grow *more*. But it will change, and you will eventually walk into the full illuminating glow of light against the dark velvet sky.

Humans cannot burn on full capacity all the time. We need periods of rest, rejuvenation, stepping back, stepping up, saying *No,* or throwing caution to the wind and trying something new. When our passions are ignited, our mystical moon light will shine in full. Like a large ball of orange delight on a breathtaking autumn Harvest Moon Night.

Strange World: A Writing Inspired by the Wolf Moon

by Amannda G. Maphies

This is a strange world in which we are living. Thankfully, I do pretty well with *strange*. I am strange. I think my kids are strange. (They think I am even stranger.) I tend to surround myself with strange people. Once strangers become friends, they still remain strange to me. Otherwise, they likely would not become friends in the first place. I successfully used a form of the term *strange* eight times in an opening paragraph of my morning musing. That, in itself, is strange. I stand corrected...*nine*.

This morning as I pulled out of my neighborhood, I turned to the left to check for oncoming traffic. The sight of the huge yellow wolf moon caught me by total surprise. It was a mesmerizing sight, and I could not help but sit there and stare, entranced by the pull of the magic glowing ball while the sun was competitively shining in the opposite sky to my right. I sat at the stop sign for minutes staring at the moon. Turning onto my familiar road headed to my familiar office, I turned around and drove through my neighborhood searching for the perfect picture-taking spot. Of course, the photos on my smartphone do little justice to the bright yellow illuminated orb in the sky. Still, I took great pleasure in chasing the moon and how surreal it felt knowing I would be late to work because I was trying to get a perfect moon shot. *How bizarre.*

Upon arriving at work and walking across the familiar isolated parking lot, I heard the most horrible sound of metal violently crashing against metal. I hurried to my warm office and looked out the window to be sure no one was injured or needed assistance. All seemed well, but for the two cars taking up residence in the road, while the frequent flow of morning traffic swerved to miss them.

I had a talk with my kids' dad (we co-parent) about our kids.

Just normal, everyday stuff. *Not really.* Nothing is normal these days. The conversations I have with others, the posts I see on social media, the stories I hear on the news when getting ready in the morning. Part of me feels as if the world has gone crazy. The other part of me is oddly entertained by the shift in *normalcy* from what I remember of my youth.

My kids are growing up in a world different than I grew up. Did my parents feel the same way when I was a child? Their only child's world was doomed to failure? There was no hope for a simple, peaceful, and beautiful existence? I wonder these things. A lot.

Something about the full moon, and a *wolf moon* at that (what does that even mean?) has me feeling more philosophical than normal. Nothing is *normal*. The only normal thing about life is the ab-normalcy that comes along with it. The shifting of tides. The strange new way of doing things. The perspective of the more life changes, the more it stays the same.

As bad a rap as social media gets, I am thankful to have a place to vent my random thoughts and feelings. I love seeing others congregate in a familiar medium and share pictures of the moon, wild animals in their backyards, funny memes about a strange man wearing mittens and at times, truly meaningful and touching essays providing beautiful perspectives on life. Facebook is not the enemy. People's egos are the enemy. I suppose this has always been the case. We are just better able to see, hear, and model it in a world where nothing is private, sacred, and treasured.

There is an ominous feeling in the air. I like to think I am perceptive and in-tune to vibes and auras which most are not. Yet, I know it is due to my over-active imagination prompting me to view myself as an owl, with a penetrating vision cutting the dark of night with razor sharp focus. Truth be told, I am more like a sloth, lying on an uncomfortable branch, waiting for something, anything out of the ordinary to happen. And when it does, I will slowly, methodically, somewhat lazily arise from my perch in a tree, take notice of the new occurrence, and give thanks for an ever-changing world, always-evolving, entertaining, heartbreaking, painstaking, and forever immersed in the incredulity of unprecedented moments in time.

Don't Wait for Home to be Perfect to Enjoy It

by Amannda G. Maphies

I love fall. I mean, L-O-V-E IT! I love Halloween, school parties, the anticipation of my kids' costumes, trick-or-treating on a chilly autumn night, spooky movies on Netflix, hot cocoa, and I love the smell (not necessarily the taste) of pumpkin spice. I love candles and chili and hot cookies straight from the oven. I love the vibrant colors of the trees, which reach their prime just before letting go.

I love children's stories about Halloween and the following festive holidays.

I love the Hallmark channel. I love putting my Christmas tree up early so I can enjoy it longer and take it down as soon as Christmas is over (because I am usually tired of looking at it by then). I love casseroles and crock pots and the smell of deliciousness wafting through the house when I get home from work. I love dark mornings and darker nights. I love anything utilizing the word harvest.

Yet.

I have this nagging feeling that arrives every year around this time. I am sure this comes from my Type-A, perfectionistic, obsessive compulsive personality disorder relentlessly screaming in my ear, "You can't decorate for your favorite time of year until you are caught up on laundry and dishes, until the bathrooms are clean, and the dining table is not piled high with kids' homework, half-finished craft projects, and unread flea market books." My ego tells me I cannot enjoy what I truly love until all my womanly, motherly, adulty jobs are done. The sad thing is, I have listened to this ridiculous, nagging, *Negative Nancy* for years.

Not This Year, Nancy!

I am going to hunt down those Halloween and autumn stuffed-to-the-brim-rubbermaids, like a hunter the first week of open season. I am going to enlist my children to assist (bribery will likely be infused at this juncture) and we are going to decorate the heck out of our house for my favorite time of year!

I will not let the dirty clothes on my bedroom floor deter me from this very real desire I feel deep within my soul. I will close the bedroom doors to my children's rooms to avoid feeling guilty for doing fun chores over necessary chores. My house, my work, my responsibilities, and my life do not have to be perfect to indulge in those things I love.

Sure, some parts of my house may look like a garage sale nightmare, with no rhyme or reason to the order in which they appear. *But guess what?* Tonight, when I sit in my favorite rocking chair for the first time nearly all day, I will see my treasured porcelain lighted haunted houses displayed on my grandmother's old chest of drawers. I will smile at that precious micro-fiber lighted scarecrow staring down at me from whatever surface I can clear off to reserve a perfect place for her to perch. I will turn the AC up and pretend it is less than ninety-some degrees outside. (Knowing the temperatures will plummet soon enough gives me proper permission to pretend.)

Last year, I left my holiday décor in full storage in my garage. Life was too busy, too complicated, too far from perfect to add one more non-essential thing to the list. This year will be different. I do not have to cross all the T's and dot all the I's. I hereby vow to myself to focus on the things that bring me joy. The small household indulgences I can look forward to at the end of each long day at work. The memories made with my children, while they are still young enough to create those lasting memories of home.

This year, things will be different. My house will look like Halloween, for better or worse. And those nasty annoying cobwebs in the corner of each room? Well, those can wait for another day. Or, perhaps I will just leave them as ambiance, adding to the haunted feel I am so keen to create in our home.

The older I get, the more I realize life will never be perfectly aligned with my expectations. And that is okay. I can still put forth effort toward those treasured parts of life which bring great joy. And let the rest fall away, just as the bright red, orange, and yellow leaves at the end of my favorite season.

Original article can be found on The Real Deal of Parenting, at:
https://therealdealofparenting.com/why-this-fall-loving-mom-is-decorating-for-the-holidays-now/

The Masks We Wear

by Amannda G. Maphies

It occurred to me yesterday afternoon, as I sat in the mid-section of the gymnasium bleachers at my sons' elementary school, anticipating their annual Halloween parade, how much masks affect our daily lives. I am not talking about the masks we are forced to wear in modern days to protect ourselves and others from Covid. I am talking about the elusive everyday masks we put on to hide our true personas from the world.

My youngest son, a third grader, wanted to dress up as *Bigfoot* for Halloween this year. His costume is adorable. It is also expensive, oppressive, hot, uncomfortable, confining, and while he was excited to be Bigfoot, once he actually wore the costume for more than five minutes, he could not wait to rip the mask off, exposing his face to the freedom of fresh air and allowing the limitation of his sight to no longer be hindered.

My oldest son, a fifth grader, together with one of his buddies, decided to be the white-faced, creepy looking, *Scream* character. Yes, the one who murders everyone else. How proud am I that my son wants to dress up as a serial killer for Halloween?! His mask, while not as adorable as his brother's, also contributed to my older son feeling claustrophobic, hot, anxious, and overwhelmingly hindered in sight.

As I surveyed the crowd of moms, dads, grandparents, aunts, uncles, friends, and other family members around me, I noticed the majority were wearing masks. Most likely because it is required in my sons' school, especially at large events. Myself, I was feeling hot, uncomfortable, and a bit suffocated as well.

Yet.

How different was this day from any other? Just because our children (and sometimes we as parents) dress up one day a year for a holiday that gives us permission to be anyone or anything other than what we really are, is it only this one day we wear masks, hiding our true identities? I know in my case it is not.

I wear a mask every day. Again, not the cloth mask required of my job, nor the mask of makeup I refuse to leave the house without. I am talking about the invisible mask I put on every morning before facing the world. The *I'm fine, everything is fine, my life feels like it is falling apart, I am anxious, worried, stressed, but I don't want to deal with it, so I will just pretend it does not exist* mask. Do you know that mask? Have you ever worn it? Perhaps the better question would be, do you ever remove the mask so the world at large, or perhaps just your inner circle, can see the true you?

"Now no one after lighting a lamp covers it over with a container, or puts it under a bed; but he puts it on a lampstand, so that those who come in may see the light. For nothing is hidden that will not become evident, nor anything secret that will not be known and come to light" Luke 8:16-17.

While we may not want our friends, co-workers, families, or even those closest to us, our children, spouses, mothers, and fathers, to know the despair we often feel, or the many worries taking up residence in our mind, how refreshing is it to know we do not have to hide from our heavenly Father. He knows what is on our hearts, minds, souls, and the weight with which we daily struggle.

Rather than a thoughtless response, such as, "I'm fine," when asked how I am doing every morning on the elevator ascending to my fourth-floor office, God knows the deep intimate struggles I choose not to share with the world. He knows and *He cares.* He wants me to come to Him for healing, refreshment, a much-needed cleansing of my soul and vessel of water for my parched lips. I do not have to wear a mask with my Lord. Even if I do, He clearly sees beyond the mask. He sees straight to the heart of all matters concerning His children.

Freedom in His prescience is the most illuminating gift on earth. The ability to speak to a savior just like you would a trusted friend. A redeemer who keeps secrets, offers wise counsel, desires to combat the worrisome and weary woes bogging us down and inhibit the passionate light Jesus so deeply wants us to share with the world.

If, like me, you don that daily mask without a second thought, perhaps now is the time to shed the inhibiting masquerade, pour your soul out to a trusted friend who wants nothing more than to see the true, authentic, fully exposed face you hide from the world. Just like the autumn leaves slowly fall from the branches to the waiting ground below, let your daily mask slide gently away, allowing the world to know and love the genuinely real you.

Photo provided by Melissa Neeb

The Weary Old Barn

by Amannda G. Maphies

Still standing tall, though tired and weary;
With many an adventurous story to tell.
Formerly full of life, movement, and activity;
This old barn could tell quite a tall tale.

The horses and cows, the kittens and pups;
So full was the life once inside.
The sheltering walls of this crumbling façade;
Just waiting with hopes for new life.

The paint on the outside is chipping away;
The structure leans just to the right.
With a strong gust of wind, it is quite possible;
The old barn will not survive another night.

Gone are the days where the farmer would come;
Milking his favorite cow.
Kittens running fast and playing carefree;
Goats nipping at clothing and jumping with glee.

Those days are all past;
The farm has been sold.
The home is abandoned;
And scheduled to be destroyed.

What will become of the old barn?
Only Father Future will tell.
The shell is still standing, a once bustling vessel;
Now weathered, rotten, and stale.

The wind silently whispers;

The old barn opens her sleepy eyes.
Could this be the day;
She sees signs of new life?

Just over the hill and down the long lane;
Is that an old tuck she spies on the drive?

What could this mean;
An updated face?
New life springing forth;
To end her disgrace?

She longs to feel full;
Inhabitants rummaging around.
An end to this utter loneliness;
A new mission profound.

An empty shell with no story to tell;
This is not the life she wants to live.
With no life within, she closes her eyes;
And silently, mournfully gives permission to the wind.

Chapter 11

Tugging at the Heartstrings

Forever and a Day

by Carrie Kendall

You're like a dream come true.
No simple song will do.
To say I want you in my life.
Forever and a day.

And a day won't go by
Without this joy in my life.
Because God answered a prayer with you.

So I promise I will love you
No matter what you do
And I promise I will always be your friend.

You can count on me for anything
And I will do my best
Because your momma will love you
Forever and a day.

From Broken to Beautiful

by Amannda G. Maphies

I recently got engaged. After a decade of pregnancy losses followed by two healthy babies, a nasty divorce, the death of a fiancé and several other life-altering events, my thirties were a tumultuous whirlwind of epic highs and devastating lows.

I met a man less than a year ago on a dating site. This man changed my life in more ways than I can express. He lovingly picked up the broken pieces of my past and glued them back together in a kind and gentle, understanding way. He loves the imperfect parts of me and inspires me every day to accept my past, relish my present, and look hopefully toward my future. What is now *our* future...

I wanted to write about the ring he gave me for our engagement. It is special on so many levels. The design was inspired by one of the greatest women I have ever known, my grandmother, Joann Dolores Mann Wadlow. I know she is looking down from Heaven with a joyful smile of thanksgiving that her granddaughter finally found *the one whom her soul loves*. This is for you, Grandma...

I look for signs. Every day, in countless ways, I seek inspired messages in the form of signs. Do I assign meaning to a totally random and likely coincidental situation? *Possibly.* Yet, if the message I see brings me comfort, peace, and a little shot of joy, there is certainly no harm. After all, the meaning attributed to anything in life is only as deep and purposeful as we give it.

This ring has a story I want to tell. I had a bracelet of my grandmother's. Truth be told, my mother owned the bracelet. I sort of *borrowed* it...with no intention of returning it. One day, I was wearing said bracelet and looked down to see one stone missing in the line of precious turquoise stones cascading the top of the bracelet. I was in a pickle, because not only did I have to tell my mother I had taken her bracelet, but I also had to explain that I somehow lost a stone (with another cracked that could fall out at any moment).

I humbly fessed up to the petty theft. She said she knew I had the bracelet as she saw me wearing it. *Oops!* Clearly, I was not meant to be a career thief...or any type of thief, for that matter.

I quit wearing the bracelet because I was afraid to lose more precious turquoise stones. The sweet bracelet sat in my jewelry box, day after day, sadly staring up at me as I chose other turquoise pieces to adorn my daily outfit. I know that turquoise bracelet, had it been allowed feelings, would have felt hurt, broken, rejected, un-useful and permanently retired from a life of glorious showmanship.

A few months ago, Justin and I started talking about the next step in our relationship. We knew we had finally found *our person* and at our age, saw no reason to wait. He asked me at one point what sort of engagement ring I would like. I really had no idea! He knew of my love for turquoise and the deep meaning this stone holds for me. He mentioned a turquoise engagement ring. I had never seen one, but thanks to Google, I found several breathtaking pieces I loved.

Justin happens to have a friend who is a jeweler. We visited with him to see if we could have a ring custom made. He said it was a possibility, but he would need to outsource the turquoise from Arizona. As elated as I was with this possibility, something did not sit right with me. I needed more personalization than a random stone from a state I have never even visited.

Late one night, I was struck by divine inspiration (possibly a message from my very grandma). We could use the pieces of turquoise from my beloved Grandmother's bracelet. We could use each piece to represent the children we have separately, that have come to be our family united as one. I was so excited at the prospect of this old, worn, broken piece of nostalgia had a new, expected and amazingly glorious purpose.

There was a time in life when I felt old, used, unwanted and *put out to pasture* like an old horse mindlessly grazing through my days, waiting to expire. (Okay, maybe that is a bit dramatic...but consider the source). I did somewhat relate to an old piece of jewelry with little relevance to its owner. *Yet.*

After years of continued healing, a strengthening of faith, a self-love to the extent I have never experienced, I became a new person. Much like the bracelet, I had a purpose. I had a passion. I had been reborn.

This particular picture is my favorite. The way the sun captures the diamond is a message to me that my grandmother is smiling down from Heaven. I imagine her shaking her head in agreement, smiling her *she's up to something smile* and winking at me in that playful way we all knew and loved, while saying, "Amannda (she was the only one that has ever called me Amannda), you were meant to shine."

Justin tells me all the time, "I wish you could see yourself the way I see you." Rather than broken with an overflowing bundle of baggage, in looking at this breathtaking, unique piece of jewelry that has a beautiful story to tell, I think maybe I do ...

Fly High Mom

by Amannda G. Maphies

Earlier this week, after a long day in the office, I decided to get my nails done. It is one of the few routine indulgences I cannot deny myself. As I was sitting in the familiar chair at the familiar nail salon, a lady walked in the door. She was talking on her cell phone and seemed a bit ... *disassembled.*

When the nail technician asked how she could help the incoming customer, the woman asked if they could do a letter on each of her nails. Intrigued, I wondered exactly what message she was hoping to convey with her obviously well-thought-out planned nail art.

Several seconds of a language I did not understand ensued by the owners of the business. Finally, the technician asked the waiting woman what letters she desired.

The stranger in the very un-private lobby thought about it for a second, perhaps gaining her composure enough to say the following, "Fly High Mom." The message seemed odd to me. Is her mother going skydiving? Is it a code for some kind of private joke she shares with her children, or a sibling? Is she rooting for someone special, a mother or mentor in her life battling some kind of illness or undergoing a major life change? My mind was racing with possibilities. And then, just when I could barely stand it, her next words pierced my heart, "My mother passed away. Her funeral is tomorrow, and I want my nails to display the message I want her to know."

As you can imagine, my curious heart turned to a sad, empathetic, broken heart for this young woman. I wanted to get up and give her a hug. I didn't. And, quite honestly, I regret not doing so.

What a message though! "Fly High Mom." Not only does it emulate the hope a daughter feels for her mother to fly high, like an angel, newly welcomed to Heaven's paradise, but it also shows a faith, a deep-seeded belief, that her mother is now in a better place.

"And he said to him, "Truly, I say to you, today you will be with me in Paradise." Luke 23:43

A place with no tears, no pain, no emotional trauma, no wondering, no anxiety, no confusion, or discontent. Her mother has been released from a broken world and it is this daughter's deep convicted belief, she is flying high, quite possibly the antithesis of lying low, as is often the case when living disheartened upon this earth.

"He will wipe away every tear from their eyes, and death shall be no more, neither shall there be mourning, nor crying, nor pain anymore, for the former things have passed away." Revelation 21:4

I will never know how this woman's mother died. Was it a sudden, unexpected, and heartbreaking, or a long-fought illness such as cancer, or even Covid? Perhaps it was an accident, tragic outcome of an unfortunate circumstance? The possibilities are endless.

How deeply grateful am I, as a Christ follower, to own the hopeful assurance that I will one day reside in the arms of my Savior! Perhaps one of the most popular and highly memorized verses in the Bible gives us this very promise:

"For God so loved the world, that he gave his only Son, that whoever believes in him should not perish but have eternal life." John 3:16

As I reflect on this stranger, whose words I cannot seem to erase from my mind, I wish her much peace, a profound supernatural comfort that comes only from Heaven above, and the blessed assurance from Jesus himself, that her precious mother is indeed...*flying high.*

The story is, Fly High Mom. It was published by Charisma Magazine (online)
August 11, 2021 and here is the link:
https://charismamag.com/spriritled-living/familyrelationships/fly-high-mom/

Voices from the Past

by Amannda G. Maphies

Years ago, I sat on the wooden floor of my little blue bedroom in the house in which I grew up on Crest Drive, in my small hometown of Monett, Missouri. My parents had decided, after sending me off to college, that it was time for them to make a move as well. *Around the corner.* Yes, they bought a house just down the street and north, right by the large cemetery I had run countless laps and immeasurable miles over the years. While I would never think of their new *old* home as my own, since I was practically grown and had moved away to college, I was so happy for them, as this home offered a large backyard for my dad to garden to his heart's content. It also offered a rich history, including an original Sear's one-room Carthage Stone home in the backyard. It was an exciting opportunity for my parents, after years of providing countless opportunities to their one and only daughter. I was overjoyed that they were finally doing something for themselves.

I did not provide much assistance with that move. I conveniently found other things to do.... study, hang out at the local mall in my college town less than an hour away, see the spook light, talk on my larger-than-life bagged cell phone, work 13 hours a week for gas and cosmetic money, spend time with my college boyfriend, you name it, anything to avoid the colossal disaster that accompanies every home move. My parents assured me they had the *heavy lifting* covered but did request that I go through the items still lingering in my childhood bedroom and either pack them up or take them out with the trash. I am sure that my college self, slightly less obtrusive than my high-school self, but not yet the sparkling personality I have become in adulthood, muttered under her breath, rolled her eyes, and sighed in distressed agreement.

I recall sitting on the floor of my childhood bedroom, against the antique chest of drawers with the pretty crystal knobs that belonged to my dad once upon a time, going through boxes of old letters. Notes from friends during class, love letters from old boyfriends. Cards of encouragement, holiday cheer, and birthday greetings from my parents. Senior pictures of friends now scattered over several states while simultaneously scattered across my bedroom floor. Those old shoe boxes held such wonderful, heart-warming memories. I laughed, I cried, I soberly thought I had reached the epitome of maturity, looking back at my formerly *immature* junior high and high school self. I held on to most of those memories, because, well...*I am a hoarder.* Anything that holds a memory, or is attached to someone I cared deeply about, is virtually impossible for me to let go. Those love letters and comedic classroom notes offered such comfort from my past, and a vaguely familiar insight to my future.

Fast forward a few years. In preparation for another move, this time to my own adult home, I started going through the boxes in my garage. A daunting task, I was nearly to the point of exhaustion, when I came across a small shoe box. Curious about its contents, I peeked inside, and found it was full of old cards and letters. Only, these cards were not remnants of my past as a young adult. These were cards, letters, notes, and photos from when my grandparents were in the nursing home, the few years they lived out before they were called to their heavenly home.

I sat on the cold, hard, concrete garage floor reading cards and letters my mother and aunt had written to my grandma while she was dealing with the ravages of Parkinson's Disease, not to mention her husband's battle with Alzheimer's Disease, just a few doors down from her own room. These letters were not comical, though they were comforting in the ways only a daughter, sister, or dear friend tries to encourage a loved one dealing with the devastating effects of end-of-life warfare. The letters offered encouragement as well as kind, gentle words, and a myriad of Bible verses, uplifting poetry, hopeful entreaties, and loving sentiments.

While the shoe-box full of memorabilia from my youth was worlds different than the shoe-box full of that from my grandparent's last days on earth, I am beyond grateful for them both. From the hilarious to the savagely weep worthy. The excitement and adventure of youth to the hope and desire for release from a life well-lived. The camaraderie of young, healthy, changing friendships to the empathy of days gone by, the distress of disease, and the longing and hope for sweet release. Both of those boxes offer a view into my past. Happy memories followed by heartbreaking ones. Holidays full of laughter followed by holidays in mourning, facing that painfully tragic missing chair around the family dining table.

There is a season for all under Heaven. Without the dark, we would not embrace the coming light. Without the pain, we would not welcome the joyful blessings that often come when least expected. The metaphorical memory trunk of my mind grows fuller by the day. I would never choose to eliminate the hard times, for they serve a valiant purpose, shining a brilliant light on the seasons of joy, which often come after that of suffering.

I welcome all precious voices from the past.

Love that Defies Death

by Amannda G. Maphies

Today would have been my grandparents' 69th wedding anniversary. Had the fates of life not stepped in, they would be sharing a pot of strong black coffee (*"the only way to drink it,"* as my grandfather preached every time he snuck me a small amount behind my mother's watchful eye). It is a wonder I ever developed a taste for coffee, considering the high-octane strength at which he brewed the stuff. In addition to their shared love of strong coffee, they would rouse each other mid-morning for some bacon, buttered (*real* butter) sourdough toast, along with my grandpa's gigantean garden-fresh tomatoes. Then they would each retreat to the den to read the morning paper or listen to the news.

They would spend the quiet day piddling around the house and then get gussied up for a nice evening out with their beloved family and friends. I never had the privilege of seeing a man look at a woman the way Charles William (who my firstborn is named after) looked at Joann Dolores (who my mother is named after). That look of adoration, pride, wonder, at times sheer frustration, but always purely untethered and unfiltered love.

Even when my grandpa's mind was cruelly held captive for years by Alzheimer's Disease, he followed his beloved bride in death mere months after her passing from this earth. I believe he knew, deep down, in his heart of hearts, despite the ravages of time on his human mind, that the greatest part of his soul was missing. His *soulmate*...my grandma.

My grandparents shared a love you do not often see in this world, much less experience at such a close, intimate level as I did growing up. Had I not witnessed it for myself, I might fail to believe it, or recognize it in my own life. But I *did*. And I *do*.

I know they are celebrating their earthly union of love in their heavenly home. Someday we will all be reunited with the greatest loves we have ever known on this earth. Until then, the memories will prevail and fill our yearning hearts with joy, sweet solace, and hopeful anticipation. Happy Anniversary, Grandma and Grandpa!

Just like the famous Randy Travis song boasts, their love beginning on earth lives on in eternity *"forever and ever…Amen."*

Fears of Being Alone

by Waylan DeBoef (9)

I am a scaredy cat when it comes to being alone. No matter how loud I am alone, I am scared. Here are three reasons why I am scared of being alone.

First, I feel insecure, and I nearly go insane. If someone sneaks up on me, I get very scared.

Another reason is I just feel uncomfortable and unsafe. I am really scared someone will try to hurt me.

The last reason is sometimes I freeze, and I cannot move my bones. It puts shivers down my spine.

How can I overcome this? I can be more social and participate in more activities.

For now, I would like to be more social. When I overcome these fears, I still plan to be social. Although sometimes I will be alone, I will just have to face my fear.

FEARS OF BEING ALONE

FEARS OF BEING ALONE

I am a scaredy cat when it comes to being alone. No matter how loud I am alone, I am scared. Here are three reasons why I am scared of being alone.

First I feel insecure and I nearly go insane. If someone sneaks up on me I get very scared.

Another reason is I just feel uncomfortable and unsafe. I am really scared that someone will try to hurt me.

The last reason is sometimes I freeze and I can not move my bones. It puts shivers down my spine.

How can I overcome this? I can be more social and participate in more activities.

For now I would like to be more social. When I overcome these fears I still plan to be social. Although sometimes I will be alone I will just have to face my fear.

By: Waylan DeBoef

216

My Son's Greatest Fear

by Amannda G. Maphies

Last night, I put my youngest son to bed on a Monday evening after a jam-packed holiday weekend. We were all exhausted from the many outings in which we indulged as a family over Labor Day. We said our usual nightly prayers and talked about the wild adventures of the day. We had traveled to the northwest hills of Arkansas to ride some dirt bike trails. This was new to my sons and myself, but we had a most excellent coach, teacher, dirt-bike extraordinaire in my fiancé, Justin.

My boys both wildly impressed me with their adventurous spirit and desire to attempt all dirt trails, jumps, berms, and all other biking dare-devil terms I have yet to master. I told my precious son, just before his sleepy eyes shut for the night, how very proud I was of him for being so bold, fearless, and excited to try something new. The bike we rented for him was a size too big, but he handled it like a champ. Despite a couple of spills, he managed to get up, dust off, and hit the trail with even more gusto than before.

This kid is an adventurer. A dare-devil extraordinaire. Whether it be climbing trees in the backyard, balancing on a fallen log over a breathtaking Colorado rushing river, playing flag football with a group of buddies he just met, or zip-lining the Royal Gorge, there is nothing I have encountered that scares this particular son of mine.

As I said my last goodnight, I looked into his sweet little face and asked, "Is there anything that scares you?" Expecting him to say *No* or perhaps indicate a nightmarish character similar to one displayed in his beloved video games, I waited expectantly for him to reply.

His innocent little face turned toward mine. His deep blue eyes bore straight into my own. A shadow crossed the face of my son and he, very seriously, and with a slight waver to his boyish voice said, "I am afraid of being alone." His answer caught me off guard and stole the very breath from my lungs. Expecting a humorous reply, but instead receiving an answer full of depth, meaning, and a very real, very raw fear that plagues many adults, including myself.

Unprepared with a proper response, I tried to comfort him and hug the fears away. However, a day later, I still cannot get his serious answer out of my mind. It haunts me with a reality I know only too well.

When I was a child, younger than my son is now, my paternal grandfather passed away. Followed less than two years by my paternal grandmother. Their deaths produced in me a fear that I believe has followed me throughout my childhood, young adult, and full-fledged adult years. I was stricken paralyzed something would happen to my own parents. As an only child, the thought of being left alone, without the two most important people in the world to care for me, was a greater burden than my young childhood self knew how to bear.

I worried constantly something would happen to my parents, rendering me all alone in a big, scary world I had no ability to maneuver. I was that child whose parents were called at 3:00 a.m. from a sleepover, because I could not turn off the worry. I was a prisoner of my own fears for many years. I still am in some ways.

Hearing this heartfelt fear resonate so deeply within my inner child from my youngest son positively broke my heart. I wanted to take the fear, the worry, the endless array of *what if's* far from him and replace them with deep assurance, calming comfort, and immeasurable security. *Only, I can't.* Being alone in this world is a very real and palpable fear. It is only with the grace, hope, and love of Jesus we can even begin to heal from this depth of intrinsic paranoia.

"Be strong and courageous. Do not fear or be in dread of them, for it is the Lord your God who goes with you. He will not leave you or forsake you." Deuteronomy 31: 6 (ESV)

My son recently decided to follow Jesus. He told me he wants to be baptized and wishes for his Pops (my dad) to do the honors. My heart overflowed with joy and pride at this decision he has made as a young man. *The greatest decision of his life.*

I know life will bring about hardship and struggle, as no one is immune to the depths of destruction humans encounter daily.

However, knowing my son has chosen to follow Jesus puts my mother's heart at ease, because I know he will have a faithful, loyal, and loving friend for all the days of his life. His very earthly life will not end in death, but transform to life in paradise with his Savior and greatest friend.

"I will not leave you as orphans; I will come to you. Yet a little while and the world will see me no more, but you will see me. Because I live, you also will live." John 14: 18-19 (ESV)

If the fears of this life leave you feeling helpless, fearful and like a prisoner in your own worrisome mind, there *is* a man who understands. A man who walked this earth for 33 years, who struggled with human emotions, crippling concerns, and paralyzing pain. This man has overcome death and destruction. More than anything, he desires a personal relationship with you.

Start by calling upon his name. *Jesus.* The very mention of this name breeds a feeling of peace and serenity. There are times I have been so heart broken, I had no words to voice the pain. Yet, saying the name *Jesus*, produced a mystical peace which surpasses all understanding; the very peace we read about in Philippians 4:7:

"Then you will experience God's peace, which exceeds anything we can understand. His peace will guard your hearts and minds as you live in Christ Jesus."

My heart hurts for this child of mine I love beyond measure. Knowing he fears a very real demon I cannot extinguish, loneliness, holds my mothering *fix it, now* abilities captive.

Yet.

While I may not be able to combat the very real fear he feels in the deepest depths of night, I know someone who can. *Someone who will.* Someone who holds the hand of my precious son tighter than any earthly being, including myself. A man who is capable of not only slaying those very real fears, but replacing them with light, hope, excitement, and a depth of knowledge. As God's children, we never have to fear being alone again. He holds his children in the palm of his hand, just as he promised in Isaiah:

[16] See, I have engraved you on the palms of my hands; your walls are ever before me. Isaiah 49:16 (NIV)

I may not have the magic answer to alleviate my son's deepest fears attacking when the rest of his family is sleeping soundly, but I know Jesus will meet this precious child at the precipice of fear.

He will carry him through the stormy winds of life and give him a peace to traverse the rocky path, which at times, seems treacherous and impassable. My sons were entrusted to my care for a short time upon this earth. Yet, their souls will reside forever in the hands of their creator, savior, and friend. That, by far, is the greatest assurance I have as a parent, a child whose heart longs for the Lord.

An abbreviated version of this piece was published in Focus on the Family Spring 2022.

Overalls in Heaven

by Amannda G. Maphies

When I started my car to go to work, my dashboard crudely reported one of my tires was low. I was unsure if it was typical seasonal pressure changes, or if there was a nail stuck in my tire (which has happened on countless occasions).

Despite being a 42-year-old full grown adult, I called my dad...*for help*. Less than two hours later, my sweet dad showed up at my office parking lot, with his trusty (and rusty) old air compressor, and filled each of my tires, obviously including the one reading low. Only he ran out of air in the compressor, so we drove to the nearest gas station, where he continued to fill each tire until they were all reading properly.

As I stood watching this man who has come to my rescue infinite times since he held me in his arms as an innocent baby years ago, air up my tires, I happened to notice he was wearing overalls. Thinking nothing of it at the time, I later saw a picture my mom had posted on Facebook, of my grandfather (my dad's dad) who passed away when I was a child.

The *one* memory I have of Grandpa Maphies involves him wearing overalls. It could be that the treasured photo hanging on the wall of my bedroom, of me as a young girl, being held by Grandma and Grandpa Maphies (with Grandpa clearly wearing overalls) is the *memory* I hold close to my heart. Whether it is the photo, or my childhood memory, I always associate men in overalls with Grandpa Maphies. Hard-working, country men, who prefer to be outdoors, getting their hands dirty doing what they love, and helping others out of tough situations.

Today happens to be Grandpa Maphies' Birthday. I cannot help but receive the blessed gift of my dad showing up to help me for the second time this week. Coincidence that my dad was wearing overalls, as my childhood memory of my grandpa automatically conjures? No, I do not believe in coincidences. I believe this was a divinely inspired message from my grandpa, to both my dad and me.

My dad is a *chip off the old block*, as some would say, of his own Father. I know Grandpa Maphies looks down from Heaven daily, nodding his fatherly approval at not only his firstborn (my dad), but his three other children, Aunt Christy, Aunt Sherrie, and Uncle Larry… as they are all pretty outstanding folks.

Today, we remember a great man. A man who wore overalls and helped others every chance he got. A man who was taken from us far too soon. But I look at his great legacy, and I am quite sure he accomplished more in his short life than most do when given double the time.

Happy Birthday, Grandpa Maphies. Someday, I will hug you…
the way I did as a child.
I wonder if Heaven has overalls?

*This piece appeared in Daily Inspired Life with Karletta Marie. Link to
original story found here:
https://dailyinspiredlife.com/legacy-of-love-inspiring-story-130/*

Blinded by the Light

by Amannda G. Maphies

As I walked out of my office for the third time this week, into the elevator, descending to the first floor, down the steps outside my building, and out onto the sidewalk, I felt something was different. Wondering about this feeling I sometimes get proceeding poignant thoughts or strange occurrences, I crossed the road and turned onto the familiar sidewalk, leading to my parking lot.

The sun was strategically placed *just so* in the sky. I was bathed in a bright, warm, radiant light, feeling like the last remaining human on earth. It may be December 5th, but I felt so warmed by the sun's glorious rays, it was as if I was walking on a beach in Fiji, instead of a sidewalk dressed in winter boots and layers of warmth, on a December afternoon in southwest Missouri.

This was as close as I have ever had to an *out of body experience*. I felt as if I could almost rise out of my physical body and see myself being smiled upon by the warm rays of Heaven. That is exactly how I felt, peaceful, comforted, giddy with euphoria, in the direct line of this bright and shining star.

Was this how Saul felt when blinded by the fiery sunlight on the road to Damascus? A light so bright and a force so strong, Saul, the Christian Killer, was miraculously blinded and transformed into Paul, the Apostle most in tune to and kindred with his Savior, Christ Jesus.

This otherworldly light shone brightly on every cell of my body. Is this what the entrance to Heaven feels like? The *Go Toward the Light* expression we often hear people respond to on their death bed.

No man has seen the face of God and lived to tell the tale. Yet, His children are welcomed to glorious eternal Eden of Paradise called Heaven when their time on Earth draws to a close. Was I graciously handed a small glimpse of that magical glow today at 4:03 p.m. Central Standard Time on a random Wednesday afternoon in December? Was it a loved one shining their love down upon me? Reminding me they are present, protective, and their love carries on even though we are separated by physical worlds.

Was it an angel providing the strength and hope I needed to get through the remaining hours of the day? Or was it simply the sun, setting at its usual wintertime appointed hour, and hitting me at just the perfect moment to embody a miraculous experience? *One I will never forget.*

Whatever it was I felt on the sidewalk this day, it was beautiful. It was magical. It was, I believe, a very small piece of sacred holiness I was blessed to receive. Thank you, Lord. I sincerely, whole-hardheartedly, immeasurably feel grateful for the gift I received on this day, bathed by the warmth and light of your infinitely eternal love.

Something Old, Something New

by Amannda G. Maphies

I recently made an homage to the special items I took to Taos, New Mexico for our recent wedding elopement on December 31, 2021. The well-known adage, *"something old, something new, something borrowed, something blue"* came in handy when planning this special adventure weeks ago.

Something Old: My grandmother's shawl. Worn and faded with the wrinkles of time. When I wrapped it around my shoulders, it was as if my grandmother was hugging me from behind. The warmth and comfort I felt knowing this delicate piece of lace and cloth belonged to one of the most precious women I have ever known, gave me such a sense of tranquility. My grandma could not hold my hand in person on this monumental day, but she daily holds my heart from Heaven. And I felt her presence on this day like none other.

Something New: This precious little snowbird wedding couple were given to me by my sweet mother. She was hopeful we could use them to top our wedding cake. Only there was no wedding cake. Still, we hung this tender ornament on the Christmas tree in the sanctuary of the tiny southwestern church with the turquoise cross, where we were married. It shone bright and lovely against the backdrop of shiny lights, tinsel, and years of collected ornaments from members of this loving church.

Something Borrowed: I borrowed several items from my Aunt Ann, but the two that stood out most to me were my grandmother's timeless pearls along with her vintage ivory clutch. The pearls symbolize class, grace, natural beauty, and the romantic innocence of fresh new love. My grandma was a graceful woman with a spicy flare. Wearing her pearls helped me to embody the woman, the wife, I wish to be to the man who stood before me on our wedding day.

Something Blue: My mother bought these earrings for me

several months ago, shortly after Justin and I got engaged. She found them in a vintage antique store, so they were not technically new, though they were new to me. With my intrinsic love for turquoise, these earrings served as a bright pop of color against the old-school vintage ivory of my dress and flowers.

While all of these treasured material items filled me with a sense of nostalgia, grace, and peace, they also served as friendly reminders on my wedding day. The old is past and gone. Mistakes made, losses felt, forgiveness granted, creating a new path of looking ahead to a future of hope and second chances. This love, this something new, walking hand in hand with my fiancé turned husband, is one of the greatest blessings I have ever known.

Something borrowed is the faith, loyalty, and companionship we have both witnessed in our parents' and grandparents' beautiful and long-suffering marriages. We aspire to be *"that couple."* The ones who last. Who cross the finish line. The companions who, no matter what life storms arise, never cease to offer their own life preserve in efforts to save their beloved partner.

Lastly, the something blue. The color of eyes we both possess. Staring into the windows of each other's soul for the next...however many years we are gifted to walk this life together. Whether with young and vibrant blue eyes, or two old and weary barely beating hearts, may the love we felt on our wedding day grow by leaps and bounds, height and depth, endlessly slashing new boundaries, until death do us part.

And then, dear husband, you must find me in eternity ...

One Single Rose

by Amannda G. Maphies

One single rose can say so much.

It can say, *'I'm sorry'* after a vicious lover's quarrel.

It can say, *'I love you'*, coupled with a promise to choose that love infinitely, day after day, until death, and even beyond.

It can say, *'Congratulations'* to a beloved friend after a big achievement.

It can say, *'Happy Birthday'* to a special someone on their special day.

It can say, *'See you in the next life'* when a devoted spouse finds themselves standing at the graveside of their soulmate, wondering how on earth they will go on...

A rose can say so much.

One single red rose.

The language of seeking forgiveness, experiencing joy, unrelenting sorrow, and immeasurable love.

It may just be the universal symbol that says it all.

One Single Rose.

Conclusion

This was my first undertaking of this caliber. *A book.* My *first* book. I had a lot of help. I am so incredibly thankful for those authors who contributed to this book. Without them, this project would not have come to fruition as beautifully as it did.

What started as a wild and crazy, hair-brained idea one chilly October afternoon in 2021, turned out to be one of the best crazy ideas I have ever had! I am part of a motherhood blog, and one day I was reading something on the site highlighting my love for autumn days, falling leaves, children's Halloween costumes and all things FALL. I immediately decided to put together a compilation of scary stories, coupled with funny stories, poetry, childhood memories, and anything/everything we enjoy at this mystical and magical time of year. The response was incredible, as apparently, I am not the only mother who absolutely loves autumn days and nights, and all the wonder, curiosity, adventure, and comfort they entail.

I am hopeful this will be a book parents and children will enjoy, preferably together. Think of it as a book of tales to bring out around the campfire on a chilly autumn night. Just when you feel scared, you don't think you can possibly go to sleep, turn the page and you will find humor making your stomach hurt from laughing so hard. Not to mention a trip down memory lane, thinking of your favorite childhood Halloween costume, or that of your children.

It is my hope this labor of love (which ironically took about nine months to complete, so I think of it as a true *book baby*) will find its way into the homes, bookshelves, and the hearts of many families who treasure this time of year as much as I do.

I had such a blast compiling these stories, some chilled me to the bone, while others brought tears to my eyes. There are many lessons to be learned from the experiences we share. This is only the tip of the iceberg, a whetted appetite, a surreal dream for possibly a second, third, and fourth edition.

After all, one can never have too much of a good thing.
Do you Dare...to feel Scared?

Contributing Authors

Jeanetta DeBoef Anderson is a wife of 26 years and mother to two adult children. She has been writing since age eight and has self-published two books. Jeanetta is a ghost blogger for a marriage/leadership ministry and is in the process of writing an autobiography, as well as two fiction books. She has lived in four different countries and has traveled all over the world; her travels inspire many of her writings, past and present. When not writing, Jeanetta enjoys music, family, cooking/baking, and nature.

Cheri Badgley is a wife, mother, "Nanny", and Corporate Accounting Manager. She has been married to her husband, Tony, for 27 years and together they have two boys, two daughters-in-law, two precious granddaughters who make her heart sing (another to arrive very soon), and two four-legged fur babies. Cheri's story is based on actual experiences when she lived in an older house and her older son, then four-years old, went through a phase where he saw "things".....at least he saw Jesus, too – he made the scary things go away.

Angel Baker lives with her husband, daughter and pets in rural Maryland. She is an avid reader, writer and lover of the outdoors. This story is special to her because 'The Old Barn' holds a special place in her heart from her youth. She has a blog on Facebook entitled, *Stories of a Farmhouse.*

Jo Anne Costello is a retired teacher from Larkspur, California, who finally has time to pursue her lifelong passion of writing. Thus far, she has finished two novels and a book of quirky short stories with plans to publish later this year. Her short stories have appeared in Mid-Century Modern Magazine and on the online platform Medium. Jo Anne and her husband believe they once shared their 117-year-old house with a child ghost. They often heard it running down the hallway and into their bedroom in the early hours of the morning. That particular ghost seems to have moved on, but Jo Anne has encountered several other mysterious and unexplained presences over the years, including the one in her story.

William A. DeBoef was born in June 2010 at Cox Hospital in Springfield, Missouri. He recently turned 12 years old and will be entering the sixth grade at Greenwood Laboratory School at Missouri State University this fall. Liam loves to play basketball (and has been playing with the same team of boys since kindergarten). He also loves video games, pizza, and his cat, Hamilton. Liam is the eldest son of Amannda G. Maphies, who collaborated this book. He was in no way strong-armed into contributing, but did so completely willingly and of his own accord…

Waylan Duane DeBoef was born in October 2012 at Mercy Hospital in Springfield, Missouri, one week shy of Halloween (his due date was actually *on* Halloween, but he was induced a week early). Waylan attends Greenwood Laboratory School at Missouri State University and plans to enter the fourth grade this fall. He enjoys flag football, helping his Pops in the garden, any type of outdoor adventure, and is always up for a fast roller-coaster or high ferris wheel ride at an amusement park. He adores his cat, Hamilton, and has his own special name for him, *Hammer.* Waylan was in no way forced into contributing to this work, he did so of his own free will…

Felicia Evelyn Morales lives in Brooklyn, New York. She is a single mother of two, 18 and 19 years of age. Felicia is a general manager at Applebee's Restaurant in Brooklyn, NY. She lost her brother twelve years ago and life has not been the same since. She looks for daily signs he is with her and is okay. Phoebe, the stray cat that often visits her backyard, provides much-needed comfort. She resembles the same cat Felicia's brother had as a little boy, which is what inspired her story in this book.

Dr. Melinda Hammerschmidt is a First Grade Instructor at Greenwood Laboratory School located on the Missouri State University Campus. She is certified in Elementary Education, Reading, Gifted Education and has a PhD in Curriculum and Instruction. Melinda enjoys writing stories about her former students from 22 years of teaching, spending time with her husband, and her family.

Carrie Kendall is a Math and ELI Special Educator in Liberty, Missouri. She and her husband have a tween and a teen and enjoy travel, board games and Cardinals baseball.

Melissa Neeb is a midwest wife, mom of two teens, writer, photographer, and artist. She loves spending time in nature with her 3 rescue dogs. You can find her work on all social media platforms @faithinthemessbymelissaneeb and @neveremptybymelissameeb.

Emily Kelso is an entrepreneur, wife, and mother of two boys, with a wickedly witty sense of humor. She enjoys embellished tales of the past with her sweet (and spicy) friend Manndi, mainly because the same stories are different each time they are told (much like men's fishing stories). She had so much fun reminiscing over the spooky night of this beloved movie tale, which you can find included in this anthology.

Gail Wadlow Maphies is a wife, soon to celebrate her 50th wedding anniversary to her husband, Duane, on August 11, 2022. She also happens to be the mother of Amannda G. Maphies, who authored and organized the compilation of this work. Gail enjoys travel, scary movies and stories, shopping, baking, and time spent with family and friends. She is also 'Grammy' to her two grandsons (also co-authors of this work), Liam (12) and Waylan (9), and mommy to her four-legged, furry doggie daughter, Bellamy and cats, Coya and Toby Tobias.

Allisha Reeves has been married for almost 18 years and is a mom to four amazing kids and *Nonnie* to two of the most amazing grandsons. She is an RN in a very busy postpartum unit and works in NICU as well. Allie loves reading and writing on the side and hopes to publish her first book in the next year.

Samantha Lyn Walljasper is a happily married, mother of four wonderful children. She works-at-home as a mom in the financial services industry; plus a certified life coach and relationship facilitator. Sam has an unprecedented love for her family, career(s), and she absolutely loves pursuing writing as a hobby. Her writing style is very broad, and she was thrilled to be included in this book (due to her passion for "the paranormal"). Samantha can be followed through *Over My Husband's Head* (@lovepoemskindof) on Facebook, and her books can be purchased on Amazon.

Amannda (Manndi) Maphies Wilkins is a wife to her husband of barely one year, Justin Wilkins, mother to her two sons, William (Liam), 12 and Waylan, 9, as well as her fur-babies, Lucy, Atlas, and Hamilton, and a freelance writer. She contributes to several online and written publications, including: *Her View from Home, Motherly, Salt + Sparrow, Daily Inspired Life with Karletta Marie, The Christian Journal, Calla Press, Focus on the Family, The Christian Standard, Ozark Farm and Neighbor,* and has been published in *Chicken Soup for the Soul Believing in Angels* (January 2022). Manndi's sons (William and Waylan – not to be confused with *the other* Willie and Waylon) never fail to provide daily entertainment, which inspires many of her writings. She also loves to write about everything from being a single mom and dating after divorce to finding love later in life, the devastation of miscarriage, the loss of a loved one, starting over, and dealing with anxiety and mental health issues (specifically her personal journey with OCD). Her pieces are lovingly filled with inspiration, encouragement, and always a touch of humor. Her motto is: *"Live a life worthy of writing about."*, which she strives for every single day.

Facebook: *Manndi Maphies Wilkins*
Facebook Author's Page: *Manndi's Musings*
Instagram: *Manndi8867*

www.ingramcontent.com/pod-product-compliance
Lightning Source LLC
Chambersburg PA
CBHW061607170626
46811CB00001B/353